Lost and Old Rivers

Lost and Old Rivers

STORIES BY ALAN CHEUSE

SOUTHERN METHODIST
UNIVERSITY PRESS
Dallas

Grateful acknowledgment to the editors of the magazines in which some of these stories first appeared in slightly different form: *Ploughshares*, *The Antioch Review*, *ACM* (*Another Chicago Magazine*), *Weber Studies*, *Chattahoochee Review*, *Prairie Schooner*, *Witness*, and *The North American Review*. Thanks to Sonya Cheuse for her assistance.

Requests for permission to reproduce material from this work should be sent to:
Rights and Permissions
Southern Methodist University Press
PO Box 750415
Dallas, Texas 75275-0415

Jacket photograph: David H. Gibson, *November Morning, Cypress Creek, Wimberley, Texas*, © David H. Gibson, courtesy of Valley House Gallery, Dallas, Texas

Jacket and text design: Tom Dawson Graphic Design

LIBRARY OF CONGRESS CATALOGING-IN-PUBLICATION DATA

Cheuse, Alan.
    Lost and old rivers : stories / by Alan Cheuse. — 1st ed.
        p.   cm.
    ISBN 0-87074-432-1 (cloth : acid-free paper)
    I. Title.
    PS3553.H436L67   1998
    813'.54—dc21   98-25210

Printed in the United States of America on acid-free paper

10 9 8 7 6 5 4 3 2 1

For Kristin

Contents

Lost and Old Rivers

The Mexican Maid

It never occurred to Birnhaus that he might clean the apartment himself. Immediately after Sara's departure he had dabbled at dishwashing and in the three months since then he'd changed the bedsheets a few times—as many times as he had had other women in the bed—but that was about it. His heart wasn't in it. A thick crust of toothpaste and sputum built up on the rim of the sink in the master bathroom and dust gathered in the bedroom like sea wrack at the baseboards and around the bottom of floor lamps, table legs, chair legs. When one night Birnhaus waited for a video to rewind he unconsciously ran his finger across the top of the VCR and noticed the deep stripe he had drawn in the dust. A few evenings after that, while reading in bed, he dozed off and let the book slip from his grasp and when he reached down to retrieve it felt something round and hard under his fingertips. This turned out to be a turd deposited there who knows when—it would've had to be some time before Sara left—by Gingerbread, the rust-colored mostly poodle his ex had brought to their marriage.

The milk curdling in the refrigerator, the mildew on the shower curtain, the mountain of newspapers that had grown next to his desk, the overflowing trash baskets, none of this had as much of an effect on him as did that single dog souvenir beneath the bed. His passions about the split-up had calmed a bit. Probably a month or two before, he would have called Sara and shouted at her until she slammed down the receiver at her end with the same rage that had driven him at his. But things had settled.

Chuck Johnson had told him they would, he of the many affairs and no marriages.

"How do you know all this stuff?" Birnhaus said to him one night over the crashing waves of voices at Paolo's.

Johnson, a few years younger than Birnhaus but with a lot less hair, sipped his tequila and looked around the crowded bar.

"Do I know that within the next ten minutes in will walk a woman with an incomparable body who we'll figure to be twenty-two and who'll turn out to be just over sixteen?"

"You don't have to be Nostradamus to figure that," Birnhaus said. "You just have to have been sitting at our table last week."

"Last week you were carrying a bigger torch for Sara than you are now. Everything runs down, Lucretius tells us. It's the nature of things." Johnson belched. He took another sip of tequila and flashed Birnhaus a grin.

A woman walked in, two women, in fact—or girls, as Birnhaus pointed out to Johnson without much glee—and they talked to them awhile and, since the bartender didn't make a fuss about it, bought them drinks.

But Birnhaus's heart wasn't in this either. A twist of Johnson's elbow in the wrong direction sent some liquid splattering across Birnhaus's shirt sleeve, something he would have laughed off when Sara was around. Now all the accident did was make him think about the pile of other soiled clothes back in the apartment, and of that hardened memento left behind by his former dog.

Later, at home, alone with the eleven o'clock news, he tried again to face up to the mess that surrounded him and rushed into the bedroom and with a series of yanking and jerking motions stripped the filthy sheets from the bed. Voices in the other room startled him, and his heart stopped racing only when he remembered he had left the television set on. He opened himself a beer, not a terrific idea since he had been keeping up with Chuck Johnson all night at Paolo's, and sat awhile after the regular newscast to watch a group of broad-faced, dark-haired Middle Easterners discuss the disastrous events in their part of the world with a calm and coolness Birnhaus wished he could maintain when thinking about his own life.

That night he slept badly, only for a few hours before awakening to find himself burdened with an erection he promptly dealt with, christening the newly spread sheets with a thick and sticky hosing of salt-perfumed sperm. Then he lay back in the odd greenish glow of his digital clock and waited for the buzzer. Birnhaus didn't have to be Nostradamus to predict that some time or other he would lift himself out of this funk. But when? When?

The alarm caught him dozing, dreaming even, or so he thought, having in his mind the fleeting memory of a walk through a seaside resort with some unknown woman, something he knew he hadn't done recently in his waking life. The conviction built in him as he showered and dressed for work. Something—something was going to have to change.

This sensation stayed with Birnhaus most of the day, during which he performed as a kind of sleepwalker the particular labors that had brought him a reasonably large amount of cash each year since he had left business school. At lunchtime, instead of grabbing a bite to eat with Johnson or one of the other men in the office, he stayed at his desk, fiddling with numbers on his screen. It was odd these days how nothing soothed him so much as playing his fingers across the keyboard, odd and rather ironic, since it had been Sara's great lament that he *couldn't ever figure anything out.*

Figure what? he'd say.

Figure it *out,* she'd throw back at him.

When everything fell apart and Sara and Gingerbread left for L.A., Birnhaus dabbled a little at figuring things out in a series of Saturday morning sessions with Dr. Gorbo, a psychologist with an office on a lower floor of his building. The location was obviously convenient and such sessions were covered in his health plan. But it wasn't long before his late Friday nights with women or even just drinking with Johnson at Paolo's won out over his desire to learn exactly what it was he needed to figure out.

"Get a little jazz in your life," Chuck said to him that night when they started at Paolo's and then met two women and walked over to One Step Down. A trio played souped-up ballads and got people tapping their glasses on the tables.

"I'd rather have a little Debussy," Birnhaus said, "or Satie. Yeah—Satie—"

A blank look unfolded on the face of the girl nearest him. Only a few weeks before, this would not have fazed him. He would have been encouraged that this woman—or girl—with streaked blond hair and a look of innocence painted over her already innocent, or was it ignorant? face, would not care much for knowing anything beyond the moment and the color of her hair and nails. Even a few weeks before, Birnhaus himself was still not much for talking except for the sort of conversation that pushed you along toward the time when you stripped away her clothing and yours and tore breathlessly to a climax.

"I'm not feeling so good," he said, offering a weak smile to his date and her friend. He set his drink down and pushed his chair back from the table. "I'm sure Mister Johnson here can keep you both happy."

"What's that supposed to mean?" said the girl with the painted face. Her voice was pettish and as she licked her lips to close off her remark Birnhaus felt a great rush of pleasure at the thought that he was about to make his exit. But in the next instant her look that seemed at first so scornful turned into a sort of smile and her tongue peeked out, lizardlike, from between her thickly made-up lips in a little lascivious farewell, leaving Birnhaus to ponder all the way home along shadowy streets broken only here and there by lamplight just what might have transpired between him and the girl if he had stayed.

No television news for him that night, no reading in bed. He dug through some of the CDs Sara had left behind to discover the Satie he was thinking of and played "Gymnopedies" loud enough to hear it in the bedroom when he threw himself into the soiled sheets and fell into a dreamless slumber. When he awoke early the next morning he found himself once again engorged with lust and ready to relieve himself even though he had vowed not to the night before.

There was only one thing to do, he decided over his coffee, in order to break up the logjam in his head and give himself some peace. So after the coffee he passed up pedaling a few miles on his exercycle, found some clean clothes amid the huge pile of unfolded laundry overflowing his dresser, and took the elevator to the second floor.

When he stepped into Dr. Gorbo's waiting room he discovered a short, wide-hipped woman with a crinkled, nut-brown face and long dark silky hair that seemed to belong to someone twenty years younger. For a moment he thought she was a patient. But then she smiled at him, revealing several gold teeth, and bent to retrieve the plastic lining from the wastebasket at the far side of the sofa, holding up for inspection the bundle of crumpled papers and used tissues as though it were a prize.

A door opened and from the inner office came the black, stick-thin Mrs. Keen, Dr. Gorbo's secretary. Within a few minutes Birnhaus had arranged to see the psychologist again and to have the Mexican maid come up to his apartment to clean once a week.

SEÑORA CLARO BRUSHED her hair from her wrinkled face and thanked him profusely when he wrote out her first check. Her breath was tinged with spices Birnhaus could not identify—cloves? saffron?—and he knew from then on when she had been in his apartment even before he saw the sparkling surfaces in the kitchen or noticed that the pillows had been carefully arranged once more on the sofa before the window, the lingering traces of those same mysterious spices tempering the astringent odor of cleanliness she left in her wake. Her English, as it happened, was good enough so that he didn't have to strain that first time when giving her instructions about the front lock—since Mrs. Keen gave her such a good recommendation he didn't hesitate to present her with her own set of keys—and though she said she would have to come at odd hours in order to fit him into her schedule it scarcely mattered to Birnhaus because of his own long days.

The one time in the next several months he came home early, he opened the door to sniff the by now familiar odor of her spicy presence and found her huffing and puffing as she struggled to pull the sofa away from the wall so that she might clean behind it. As he put his own weight into the labor, he graciously ordered her never to try that again, and then laughed with her as she held up the woman's scarf that she found on the rug beneath where the sofa had stood.

"It was my wife's," he said, but in truth he didn't recognize the scarf.

"It's uh-very beautiful," said Señora Claro, catching her breath after the laughter.

Birnhaus couldn't be sure if she was praising the scarf in order to pay him a compliment about Sara, or if she merely liked the scarf.

"Please take it," he said, folding her hand over her discovery.

"Oh, no, señor," said the Mexican maid, but it was clear she was accepting it as a gift.

Hiring the maid or seeing Dr. Gorbo again—Birnhaus couldn't have said for sure which of these decisions made him feel better about his life until one Saturday a few weeks later when he awoke with that same young blond girl in his bed whom he had skipped out on that night at One Step Down. Janine was her name and she was twenty-three, which gave Birnhaus a full ten years on her. He should have gotten dressed and gone downstairs for his appointment, but instead he dawdled in bed with the girl and then dozed off, dreaming that same dream again about walking with the woman by the seawall.

Janine had gone by the time he awoke. A shopping trip with her girl friend so-and-so, her note told him. In an odd new way, Birnhaus felt happy she had left, although he admitted to himself she wasn't much of a presence when she was with him, not being much more than her body and her makeup and her youth. Into the bathroom—and he was pleased with how clean the commode and sink and shower stall showed under the lights. Something pricked at his toe just then and he bent down to retrieve a barrette Janine must have dropped as she was making her escape. He stared at it and then dropped it into the plastic-lined wastebasket beneath the sink.

A few minutes later he called downstairs to apologize to Mrs. Keen for missing his appointment and asked to reschedule. There was a sternness in the woman's voice he didn't appreciate, until she changed her tone to ask how Señora Claro was working out.

"Fine," he said, "just fine."

And it was true, she was working out splendidly, vacuuming and scouring and dusting each week so that Birnhaus came to look upon himself as a man who lived in cleanliness rather than amidst filth and debris. Now and then—miracle of miracles—he even stopped off at the supermarket on the way home and picked up some ground beef or chicken thighs and cooked for himself, feeling free to splash about with sherry and oils because the señora would be in within a day or two to clean up the mess.

"You were right," he said to Chuck Johnson one night at Paolo's as he raised a glass in his direction.

"About what?" Johnson flashed a foolish grin at the girl at his side.

"About fucking everything. You're a genius. Bald—but a genius."

Johnson gave him the finger. The girls laughed. This was the way things went for months. They drank a lot and then later in the evening went their way two by two, Johnson and his girl to his place, a fancy little efficiency over near Dupont Circle, and Birnhaus and his girl, first Janine and then a secretary named Kara, a freckle-spattered redhead from West Virginia, to his fresh-smelling quarters.

The season changed, which meant that now and then they might have to take a taxi to avoid the cold rain, and once or twice Birnhaus even cranked up his old BMW which was parked most of the time in the garage below the building. The city, he had concluded long ago, was meant for walking and taxis and now and then a Metro ride. He and Sara had taken an occasional weekend drive into Virginia, but somehow Birnhaus wasn't moved to travel anymore, not, at least, with the girls he was going out with these days.

He talked of Sara once in a while. At a session with Dr. Gorbo before he let the therapy thing slide again, he put it this way: "I hadn't been thinking about her, you know? and then one night I was reading in bed, yep, I still stay home a few nights alone, reading, watching a movie, maybe, so anyway, there I was, and I turned a page, this was in a spy novel by Robert Littell, somebody you really ought to read, an old school pal of mine turned me on to him, anyway, so I was reading and that was when I remembered falling asleep with a book one night a few months after Sara left, and I woke up, you know how you sort of snap yourself awake? and I reached down for the book, it fell under the bed, you know? and I touched this hard thing, a turd from our old dog, a little doggie souvenir, and the other night I was in bed again and like I said I turned the page and I remembered that other time . . . and that was when the thoughts of Sara came back to me. Can you believe that? because I was remembering finding that dog turd? But I don't find shit like that anymore, oh, yeah, a bad pun, I didn't mean it, but anyway I have this woman who comes in to clean, the same woman cleans this office, as a matter of fact, Señora Claro, and she does a great job. I love coming back to a clean apartment. To tell you the truth, Sara just never got the place all that clean, or how else do you think that dog turd stayed there under the bed? . . . I miss that dog now and then, you know. When Sara left I felt a little sting about her going. I don't think she felt anything. According to her, she was just beginning to have a hard time with me when she packed up and left. That's how Sara always did it. Trouble coming up, she splits. She learned it from her father. He abandoned the family a couple of times and came back and left again before he died. But that's Sara's family, and I should be talking about mine, right?"

Yet he scarcely ever did speak of them, dead father, mother remarried and living outside Minneapolis, while the sessions with Dr. Gorbo continued, which was only for a few weeks more. As it happened, work began to pick up, three or four turns he suggested that the company take proving to be enormously successful and distracting him from the vague unease that had sent him to see the psychologist in the first place. And then a new woman turned up, too, a Jewish girl from New York, a friend of a girl Chuck Johnson was going out with, and she took the train down to see him several weekends that winter.

It was the night before one of those weekends that Birnhaus came home to a dusty apartment. The following Monday the mess he and the girl from New York had made was still there when he returned after dark. Another two days went by and he began to get antsy about Señora Claro's absence. By Saturday morning he was feeling annoyed. He wanted to call Dr. Gorbo's office to ask about the Mexican woman, but of course he didn't want to speak to Mrs. Keen. He decided to let it slide one more weekend, but the place was getting so filthy—and he had grown accustomed to the opposite state—that he lasted only to the middle of the week.

Mrs. Keen was merciless with him on the telephone, as he knew she would be, explaining with ice-cold precision that Señora Claro had developed a heart problem and gone in to the Washington Hospital Center for a catheterization. No, she didn't know when she would be back to work again, though she supposed it would be as soon as possible.

"She supports all of her sister's family down in Mexico," Mrs. Keen said in a voice that Birnhaus could scarcely hear without wincing. "So I'm sure she'll be back just as soon as the doctors tell her it's okay to work again."

All right, all right, Birnhaus was thinking, but at least she didn't bring up the subject of another appointment, and then they had finished, and Birnhaus found his finger, nearly unbidden, punching out another number.

"Hey, how's the pup doing?" he said when Sara came on the line.

"Norm," she said, "what a surprise. But I can't talk to you right now. Can you call back tomorrow?"

"Sure," he said, trying to keep his disappointment to himself. Seated as he was at his desk, he immediately began to fiddle with the keyboard, but then he set it aside and called Chuck's extension but the line was busy. He was tempted to call Mrs. Keen again to see if she had Señora Claro's home number, but then Chuck himself wandered over and they made plans for the evening. Chuck had an appointment with his dentist just after work so they decided to meet at Paolo's later on.

At about seven o'clock Birnhaus came home to find his door open a crack. His heart pounding from his initial fear of burglary, he peered inside, and after listening carefully, pushed the door a little further and stepped into the apartment only to discover Señora Claro standing at the kitchen sink wielding her sponge. Birnhaus stood a moment and talked with her, trying to calm himself, pleased to be inhaling once again the familiar odor of cloves and the other spices the woman chewed. He inquired about her medical problem and learned that she had been been catheterized and that it would be necessary for her to go back again for further scrutiny within the month.

"And have they put you on a special diet?" Birnhaus was staring at her throat and it was only then he realized that tucked into the top of her plain white blouse was the scarf he had given her.

"Oh, eh-yess," she said, showing him her gold teeth in a smile. "Es-special diet. No meat, no fat." There was a little tremor in her voice, and it might have been her normal way of speaking or it might have been born of fear at her condition.

"They eh-think I need an *operación*," she said, her brown face crinkling into a leathery but pleasant smile as she resumed her wiping of the kitchen surfaces.

Birnhaus wrote out her check, and after a brief pause wrote a second check, which, he explained when handing it to her, was to help her with any untoward medical expenses.

"Gracias," said Señora Claro, pausing to stuff both checks into the pocket of her brown polyester pants.

"I'm going out now," Birnhaus said.

"Sí," the woman said.

"And remember," he said, pointing to the sofa and making a pushing motion with his hands and arms, "no moving furniture. *Capeesh?*"

"Sí, Mister Birnhaus, I won't eh-push." She showed him those teeth again in a smile.

So Birnhaus left for his rendezvous with Chuck Johnson, feeling celebratory now that the maid was back.

"What's with you tonight?" Chuck said after a few drinks, though Birnhaus could hardly find the words to explain. And within the hour he was too drunk even to try. So they decided to put their energy to the best possible use and call some girls.

Janine had her answering machine on and didn't come to the telephone. The redheaded, freckle-faced girl from West Virginia was at home but already in bed.

Johnson finally hit the jackpot with a call to a new girl, a black secretary from his part of the office. Her name was Delly, and she and her roommate were just sitting around watching a movie and though they didn't want to come out, they invited the two men over for a nightcap.

"It's a different life-style," Johnson said in the cab on the way over to Adams-Morgan. "It's passed down from generation to generation. Their ancestors, see, were kept up real late toiling in the fields, so staying up late just became a way of life in America."

Birnhaus was trying to catch his breath, because his heart was racing uncharacteristically fast and he was pondering this bit of social interpretation when they reached the apartment house where the two girls lived.

But it turned out to be three girls.

"Our cups runneth over," Johnson said, putting his arm around Delly as soon as they came in the door.

Birnhaus thought Delly was cute, her skin the color of mahogany, not much different from that of Señora Claro. And she had a pert, Indian-like nose, and a great smile—no gold teeth—he wondered why he hadn't noticed her before in the office. Beside her the other two girls seemed dark and drab despite the brightness of their bathrobes and hair ribbons and smiling faces.

Chuck ordered a couple of pizzas and they ate these with a large quantity of beer and watched the last half of *Pretty Woman*, laughing and talking. Birnhaus sat on the sofa with Delly, and enjoyed it immensely, especially, toward the end of their stay, when he conjured up the little fantasy about what might happen if and when he asked Delly out for a drink.

The nip on the ear she gave him just before he and Chuck went out the door was all the incentive he needed to decide to ask her out for lunch the next day. The problem was that by the time he got a cab and went home and took the elevator to his floor he had forgotten her name.

What was it? he interrogated himself as he took out his keys and unlocked the apartment door.

The living room lights were ablaze, a welcoming touch left by the Mexican maid, and the air was filled with the odors of cleansers and the familiar scent of her spices. Birnhaus smiled as he went for the telephone, hoping to extract the black girl's name from Johnson before his friend fell asleep.

"You asked her?" Chuck said at the other end of the line. His voice was blurred, as though the connection were made under water or he had suffered a stroke.

"You're not pissed, are you?"

"I'm pissed," Johnson said.

"It's just for lunch," Birnhaus said, glancing around the room and admiring the tidiness of it all.

That was when he noticed her, wedged between the television set and the wall, crumpled into a jackknife position, as though she had been bending over either to pull out the plug or put it in when the attack came upon her.

"Señora!" Birnhaus cried out, dropping the telephone and rushing to her side. He knelt and tried to turn her body toward him.

She was very heavy. Remembering some vague instructions from a course he had heard about but never taken in college, Birnhaus with some effort pulled the woman away from the wall and turned her on her back in the middle of the rug. He clumsily undid the clothing around her chest, tearing at the scarf, pulling open her cheap synthetic blouse. Her brown chest was nearly as flat as a man's and only the dark fleshy stubs of her nipples gave him pause before he began massaging her with his palms, pressing hard with his thumbs.

He heard a squawk and at first thought it was the woman, until he remembered the telephone and lunged toward the fallen receiver.

"Chuck," he said, "call an ambulance," and then raced back on his knees to the woman's side. Leaning close to her mouth he breathed in the faint familiar odor of her spices and, nearly gagging, pulled back for a moment before dipping his head toward her again, using his fingers to pry open her cold, unyielding lips, then pressed his own against hers.

Taking a deep breath, he blew in, and pulled back as he pressed down on her chest. And then with a breath he dove toward her lips again, tasting beneath the layer of spices a bitter sip of oily food and a harsh dab of tobacco. Was she a smoker? How could she do that to herself when she had such a terrible heart condition? Blowing in, pressing down, blowing in, pressing down, these thoughts raced through his mind while he labored above her inert body.

He couldn't have said how long this went on—breathing, blowing, pressing, breathing, blowing, pressing, as though he were some grotesque mother bird and this woman beneath him the nestling he was feeding mouth to mouth—but then he heard the sirens in the street below, and something caved in within his own chest, and he paused in his work above the body, panting, weeping, groaning, and somehow at the same time savoring in his own mouth the spices the woman had chewed, the meals she had eaten, the cigarettes she had smoked.

There came a pounding at the door, and as if that were the signal he was waiting for, Birnhaus collapsed onto the woman even as his gorge rose and he spewed forth his own late supper and all the beer and—it seemed—all of the drinks he had drunk at Paolo's, all of the meals he had taken there and at other exotic restaurants, and all of the smokes and the hors d'oeuvres and the snacks and desserts, and candy and medicine and syrups and toppings and the saliva of a thousand kisses, from his mother's to those on the lips of every woman he had ever tasted, this wretched acid gush of waste that flowed down over his shirt and poured onto the prone body of the Mexican maid, sloshed over her chest and neck, and left an indelible stain on the rug beneath her.

At least it seemed as if it would never come out. After the paramedics left, Birnhaus walked in circles around the stain for what seemed like an hour, and he suddenly dashed into the kitchen and went digging beneath the sink for cleansers and soaps and sponges and brushes and went to work on the mark on the rug. Wetting, washing, scrubbing, staring, studying, and then beginning the cycle again, he spent the last of his energies of the day—or night, for it had been night a long while now and was edging up on the deepest part of itself, when blackness is compounded on blackness and, in this part of town, the air is still and no birds sing. When he flung himself onto the bed, the last image he held in his mind before going under was the outline of the stain. Nearly circular, but with ragged edges, it might have been the circumference of some exotic country on a map in a yellowing geography book.

Someone from the police called the next morning—on the telephone, not in person, because they had too many homicides to deal with these days, the woman said, and they were stretched thin enough to have to telephone rather than make a trip out into the field over a death by heart failure. He repeated his story and the woman seemed satisfied.

"We'll get back to you if we find we need any more information, Mr. Birnhaus," she said by way of farewell.

Birnhaus stayed at the telephone, first calling the office to say he would not be coming in today. Then he tried dialing downstairs but got only the answering service. His heart was beating fast and his breathing seemed a little troubled, his nose stopped up. Was he coming down with something? That was a possibility. Or could it be all the dust in the apartment that was stopping him up? The señora, may she rest in peace, had not finished her work. He wondered how he might go about finding someone else to clean for him, and then hated himself for the thought. But in the elevator—not a long ride, though longer than it usually seemed— he couldn't help but wonder about a replacement for his cleaning woman.

I'll ask Mrs. Keen, he decided, since he had to break the news to her anyway. If she wasn't in yet, he'd just sit in the hall and wait.

Sniff, sniff, he tried to breathe normally through his clogged nostrils. Nothing doing. Sniff. Snuff. Sniff.

He had some questions for the doctor, too.

Midnight Ride

Where did I get the idea for this movie? It was the year of El Niño—the current, I mean, and not anything else that I knew about at the time—and the meteorologists were telling us to expect strange events in the atmosphere.

They didn't say anything about events at home where it hadn't been good between me and my roommate Gary for over a month now, ever since one of our late-night script sessions turned into a mistaken encounter in my bedroom. Still, except for the color of the sky—low clouds, smog, the kind of weather we don't usually advertise, especially when it comes in the middle of summer—it was lovely outside that afternoon, warm, with an inviting breeze blowing up over the bluffs from the ocean. It was that same wind that pushed all the crappy air back up against the mountains east of the city, and when you drove up to the top of the road and looked down in our direction you could see it hanging there like some slightly soiled yellow scrim someone had tacked up over the hills. From that hilltop, I wound my way down into the adjoining neighborhood and threaded the car—my old VW Rabbit—along through four or five more additions all the way to the mall. I didn't like driving the freeways much, because I always thought of Joan Whatshername's heroine Maria and the way she drove and drove, played by Tuesday Weld. That's how you get out here—probably all over America, since I don't feel much different about it than I did when I was living in Illinois—seeing life in terms of movies. Or a better, more truthful way to put it, seeing life *as* a movie. That's what it felt like when I pulled into a parking space at the mall and who should drive up alongside me but my favorite actress friend Bunny?

"Yo, Bee," she said, rolling her window all the way down. She was wearing shades and had bound her long hair up in a snood—a sort of Sunset Boulevard look. From her lips dangled the usual cigarette. I hadn't seen her since Gary and I had gone to one of those chamber music evenings over at Milt Markowitz's. I think she had been going out with the viola player in Milt's group. I remember saying to Gary, that girl looks almost like my little sister Harriet—except Bunny could never live in the Chicago suburb where Harriet and her banker husband have settled, with two kids, a dog (though no cat), and behind the house a little pond with a rowboat—but Gary was too busy flirting with the viola player himself to pay much attention.

"So, you two ready for it?" Bunny said, puffing out a little smoke from between her teeth in that schoolgirl way—what a schoolgirl!—that Gary had said, correctly, was so right for the part of Harmon Root, the runaway rich girl in the carnival story we were pitching at that time.

"Ready for what?"

I locked my car and slouched over to Bunny's window, leaning over the way you see the CHPs do along the freeway when some poor jerk has screwed up the traffic. Her perfume—it was Calandre by Paco Rabanne—twisted my nose into a knot.

"Our big dinner tonight," Bunny said.

When I looked blank, she said, "You don't remember? Roger and Balu Maginnes?"

"Shit, how could I have forgotten? But I did!" What? Was I crazy, or just depressed? Roger and Balu weren't a pair whose invitations you took lightly—the big bald producer with the drop-dead-beautiful actress wife was how I first noticed them at that same evening at Milt's house, and I remember how my heart started to flutter like a little bird in my chest when I got introduced to them.

"I'm amazed Gary didn't say anything to you," Bunny said as I pulled back from her window and looked around at the gray-orange sky.

"He was lost in his cowboy script," I said. "*Showdown at the Gay Corral.* I'm the one who should have remembered. Our big chance to pitch our carnival story again! We thought it was dead!"

"So go inside and you'll buy something to cheer you up and we'll charm them tonight. A nice shirt, maybe? That's my thing when I'm down in the dumps. A shirt. Or maybe a scarf? I don't know you so well, Bee. Are you a scarf chick?"

"No," I said. "I'm a cat person. When things get tough, I go and buy something for my Meow."

"I'm glad you like animals," Bunny said.

"You are? Why?"

And she gave me a mysterious smile and said she'd see us tonight, and with a little wave drove off along the parking lot lane toward the roadway.

I walked slowly across the lot, a vast metal beach of gleaming sports cars and sedans, and wandered along the walkways of the mall, strolling from shop window to shop window—the leather dresses and velvet coats and platinum-rimmed eyeglasses, gloves made from the skin of antelope, emeralds and rubies in the most bizarre settings, ropes of pearls, and telescopes and video phones—you name it. I found a juice bar, drank a papaya smoothie for lunch. There was a pet store, of course, and I went in and bought a little ball of catnip on a string for Meow. And then I saw another shop, where the brightly lighted window was filled with stuffed lambs and rabbits and bears. Like a sleepwalker, I made a purchase.

Then I drove back along the way I had come, the blue blaze of the ocean on my horizon, the curtain of smog behind me, and this sort of gave me hope, though for what exactly I couldn't quite figure.

I wanted to share my good feeling with Gary when I got back, except he had gone out, leaving a note on the front table saying that my mother had called.

I took out the little gift I bought for Meow and tossed her the ball. It didn't take but a few seconds for her to begin tearing around with it on the rug, crazed with the scent of the catnip. So having made at least one creature happy, I dialed my mother's number.

"I called you earlier," she said after picking up on the first ring.

"I got the message, Mom."

"It shouldn't always be my call that makes you call me."

"I'm just a wayward daughter," I said.

"Don't talk that way, Bee. If you say something, you could make it happen."

"That's sort of a primitive way of thinking, Mom."

"I don't know what you're talking about. Tell me, have you been getting around?"

"Getting around?"

"Have you been seeing any nice young men?"

I held the receiver at arm's length. Outside the window a stray gull swept from the beach on a lifting wind. It swooped past our orange tree and then disappeared at an angle into the otherwise empty sky.

"I don't get out much, Mom," I said, "because I stay at home and work. With Gary. We—"

"Friends are friends, Bee," she cut in, "but I don't have to tell you that you're not getting any—"

"Younger?" I said.

"If you've heard me say this often enough to know it by heart then you ought to know enough to believe it by now. I don't mean to nag, darling, but woman to woman I have to tell you that when you get to my age, you won't be able to look back on your work and get much comfort from it."

I took a deep breath and said, "You're right. I should have some children that I can call on the phone and make miserable because I'll be alone and pissed off at—"

"You mustn't talk to me like that, Bee."

Another breath. "I'm sorry. You don't bring out the best in me when you raise this particular subject."

"Well, tell me, then, have you seen any movie stars lately? You're always telling me about seeing people like that at lunch, Bee."

"You just shut off one thing and pick up another just like that?"

"I thought you wanted me to stop talking about the other thing."

"I just want to have a talk with you, Mom. In a pleasant way. You know, like, 'How are you?' and 'How was your day?'"

"Family isn't always pleasant in that way, Bee."

"So why do you want so much for me to start one?"

I could hear my voice sail into the highest register.

I WAS STILL close to tears when Gary came in the door. He was wearing his usual jeans and thin T-shirt with his cigarettes rolled up in the right sleeve. But despite that tough-guy stuff and his wispy moustache, he still had that little-lost-dog look.

"Have a nice shopping trip?" he said.

Right on cue, Meow came tearing through the room with her catnip ball, did a roll, and a leap, and another roll, tossing the ball of herbs and then catching it again before it came to a stop.

"My big purchase," I said.

Gary looked puzzled. "Did you call your mother?"

"That's why my eyes look red."

He came and peered into my face. "Ah, so. Well, she's at it again."

I rubbed my nose with my fist and turned away.

"At the mall?" I said when I looked back at him.

"Uh-huh?"

"I saw Bunny."

His tongue peeked out from between his teeth, the way it does when he's working on a line of dialogue and you know even before it comes out of his mouth that it's going to be a snapper.

"Oh my God. That's so dumb of me! I just remembered! But I can't go. I've got a date."

We were standing there looking at each other when the telephone rang. It was Bunny. "Better wear pants," she said.

When I hung up, I turned to Gary.

"Did you know?"

"Know? Oh, about the ride?"

I nodded.

"Yeah," he said. "I mean, I knew, but then I forgot about it. Look, Bee, if you want me to go with you, I'll break my engagement."

I shook my head. "I can do it myself. I just need to rest," I said. "Before I go."

And so I left him standing there. I went into the bedroom and lay down, feeling a little dizzy at the thought of what was to come. There's one thing Prozac does, though. No dreams. At least not for me. I touched my cheek to the pillow and went out.

THE NEXT THING I knew Meow was purring furiously in my ear, and I sat up to see the sky outside turned to lavender and fading crimson. "Hi, little Puss," I said, a croak in my voice as I ran my fingers along her back. It was late, I was sweating, but it wasn't the middle of the night so I couldn't just turn over and go back to sleep. So I hauled my butt out of bed and dragged myself into the shower. In thirty minutes, I was driving down the Ventura Freeway, heading south. The traffic began to slow and I thought to myself, Oh, girl, here it comes, this is why I hate these roads, and then I saw the orangey flickering on the horizon and figured that someone else had bigger troubles than my own. After the next curve I could see the dance of fire on the other side of the road, lower than the palm trees, higher, much higher than the retaining wall.

Two cars were burning like slabs of meat on a grill and the small auxiliary fire truck that had pulled up beside them wasn't doing much to put out the flames. Inching along on my side of the freeway those of us moving away from the accident could see the rolling lights and hear the wavering whine of the sirens of more engines approaching. God help the passengers if they were still inside! I rolled down my window and tried to look back, but our lane was moving too fast to do more than get a good whiff of the smoke. It stayed with me all the way to the restaurant, Cactus Cantina, in Burbank, surrounded on either side by stables, dark animals milling about in the corrals, steeping the air around the place with odors different from the rest of the city.

Two rows of faces greeted me inside the restaurant. There was Bunny, sitting between Roger and his beautiful blonde wife. A half dozen couples I didn't know, and Milt Markowitz, filled out the table.

"Your friend Gary called to say you were going to be late. So I had the idea we could play the old switcheroo." Milt spoke in that appealing Long Island nasal voice of his. "I'm not into punishment and I don't know if I can make it back."

Seeing my puzzled expression, Bunny piped up, "Milt rode with us, but he'll drive your car home for you and take a taxi from there if you ride his mount back over the mountains."

"I love what she said. My mount! My mount! I love that word!" Milt looked up at the papier-mâché piñatas dangling from the ceiling.

"When you didn't show at the stables," Bunny said, "I gave up on you. I'm glad you remembered where to meet us."

"Me, too," I said, noticing that Roger Maginnes was smiling up at me while his wife dabbled with her spoon at some dessert.

"My mount! My mount!" Milt kept on. "I love that word. My *mount!*" He paused and took a breath. "Except I had a saddle with teeth and it chewed up my *tuchas!*"

"The white Rabbit," I said to him as Maginnes's wife looked over at me and I turned away to dig into my bag for my car keys.

"The bronze-colored mount," Milt said to me when he lifted the keys from my hand.

Next thing I know, people are pushing back from the table and tossing their napkins onto their used dessert plates and Roger Maginnes is saying at the top of his voice, like a character in a picture he's much too subtle to make, "Troop, mount up!"

In the corral behind the restaurant I met my mount, a chestnut mare named Madonna. As the groom held her reins, I stared at her in the light of the spots above the stable door, feeling her edgy vitality under my fingers as I stroked her flank, though I went a little weak in the knees, probably because of the pungent smell. The young Mexican groom motioned for me to mount, and as I hoisted myself into the stirrup, I felt his hand pushing upward on my ass and then I was sitting high in the dark, the big animal twitching menacingly beneath me. Roger Maginnes pulled next to me sitting atop a huge black gelding.

"You've done this before, right?"

"At my friend Honey Cartwright's house every summer when I was a girl," I said, watching as his horse shimmied sidewise and then jerked away forward, but not before I caught a glimpse of the round white globes of the gelding's eyes.

Honey! I hadn't thought of her in years and years, her big house north on the lakeshore, what we used to do after dark with the black grooms from the inner-city neighborhoods. Grooms! It had never occurred to me until now what richness lay in *that* word!

The other horses, jittery, snorting, stamping in the dust in the dark, moved with a clatter out of the corral.

"Troop! Foh-ward!"

"Roger," I called after him, "you should make a Western!"

Now if you have ever wondered—and I myself certainly hadn't before this evening—just how a posse of folks on horseback would take a ride across Los Angeles, here is how you do it. The first thing is you cross the freeway, and you do this by means of a long dusty trail that curves away from the stables and declines gently toward the racing lights and roaring vehicles on the road and ducks beneath the road into a long tunnel swirling with dust and clanging with the rebounding sounds of hoofbeats. This was our first ten minutes, and my mouth clogged with the thick choking clouds we kicked up as we moved along with only the faint glow of arc lights at the other end.

Coming out of the tunnel was like coming up for air after a long dive. I took deep gulps of fresh wind, snorting along with the horses and giving myself over to the batting rhythm of Madonna as she chugged along, bouncing me mercilessly in the saddle. I looked ahead for Roger but all I saw was the huge rump of his mount as he and a couple of others took advantage of the flat stretch between the road and the hills to make their horses race.

"Hey-yo!" Voices drifted back to me over the clatter of hooves. And then we began climbing.

"It's beautiful," I called out near the crest of the trail, catching up with Bunny, who bounced along smartly atop a broad bay mare.

"You having fun?" she said.

"I'm having a ball."

Roger just then turned his horse back toward us, and in the faint glow of the quarter moon, I could see a strange smile pass across his face.

"There's that, and there's that," he said, nudging his beast into a graceful turn and coming up beside me. He pointed up at the sliver of moon and then at the trail that opened into a field of odd machines and smoking pipes poking up out of the ground.

"What's that?" I said, staring at his dreamlike landscape.

"Methane farm," he said. "These hills were built up out of garbage. As it decays it gives off methane gas."

"We're riding across mountains of garbage?" I watched now with fascination at the little puffs of smoke that burst from the ends of the buried pipes.

"You got to look the other way. It's all a metaphor," he said. I'd never heard anyone in the business, except for Milt, talk about anything like it was poetry. "They pile it on here, and it makes a mountain, and then we

ride over it and catch the view. I mean, look at that down there, Bee."
Roger pointed to where the dark hill fell away into the vast ocean of illu-
mination below us. Whatever he meant by what he said, I couldn't take my
eyes off that luminescent plain fluttering with bursts of bright lights here
and there—in which somewhere that fire I saw on the way over or another
fire in another part of the city or a fire that would burn before I knew it was
adding to the glow. Our horses held fairly still, only their occasional snorts
and heaving breaths breaking the silence up here, while faintly in the
distance at the bottom of the great decline the tiniest whines of sirens and
the rumbling of the freeway drifted up to our ears.

"Bunny," Roger said, "would you ride up ahead and see how they're
doing?"

"Sure, pardner," Bunny said, throwing me a strange look—the moonlight, however faint, clearly showed her arched eyebrows and puckered
mouth—and then peeling away up the trail.

"Bee?" Roger urged his horse closer to mine so that he could reach
over and take my mare's bridle.

I was surprised at this.

"Did I do something wrong?"

"You're so cool, Bee," Roger said. "Loosen up a little."

"What are you talking about?"

He somehow got his horse to edge even closer, so that when he leaned
across his neck, it was almost as though we were sitting together on some stiff,
old-fashioned upright divan and his head was nearly resting on my shoulder.

"Don't misunderstand," he said.

"What?"

"In my position, I could get misunderstood. There's always girls, you
know." He nodded toward the dark, and I thought that he might have
meant something about Bunny. "That's not what this is about."

"What is it about, Roger?"

Madonna jittered in place, nervous to walk, I figured. Uncomfortable
wouldn't describe what I was feeling then.

"Troop's got to get moving," he said.

"Yeah, we should."

"So?"

He tried to reach for me, but my horse backed away, spooked a little by his sudden move.

"Easy, girl," he said.

"Who are you talking to, Roger?" I said.

"Very funny," he said, turning in his saddle and looking up the trail into the darkness where all the other riders had disappeared. "But we should talk."

"I think we should."

Madonna calmed down again and I felt good sitting so high up on her, as still as the stillest part of the big mass of her body.

"I think we could talk," Roger said. "Bunny says that you have a treatment."

"That's right, pardner," I said.

"I think we can talk." Roger's gelding shied just then at some invisible menace in the dark, stamping back a few paces and letting out a blubbery snort.

I remained still, and in that moment Madonna took it upon herself to gush out a long hot stream of particularly pungent flow, the sound of which rushed through the space between Roger and me.

"We'll talk," he said, and gave his mount a kick that sent horse and rider charging up the trail.

"Wait for me," I called, digging my heels into Madonna. I might as well have been urging a statue to move. "Come on, girl!" I shouted, kicking harder as Roger disappeared into the blackness up ahead.

And then the dark kicked back, because at that instant terrible cramps nearly folded me over double in the saddle, and I sat there in agony, unable to get the horse to budge. Tears rolled down my cheeks.

"Jesus!" I called into the dark, alone up here, and really hurting. For a moment the only sound after my voice faded away was the gentle hissing of the methane tubes and the faint tumult of the city below, a whirring, shushing sound that branches make stirred by a forceful wind. My insides twisted around and knotted up. Oh, Mama! I started to really cry. Somebody please come and help me!

I looked up to see mist passing before the moon, the chill of it all settling over me like the gauzy curtain before a big empty screen.

And then it came to me, right then and there, just what a scene it would make! The girl, stranded out here on horseback, her guts churning—but why? not just like me because she had cramps, though I was thankful that my period had arrived at last, but something else, what? like maybe she was pregnant and was going into premature labor? but then why would she even think about going on a ride like this? wait, because she wanted to lose the child? because . . . she was carrying one man's child—say someone like Roger? and wanted to marry the other, say Gary, if he weren't gay? but how would it go? how would it go? and who is she, anyway? rich girl on her own horse? or working girl on a rented mount? a career girl from the Midwest, say? who came out to work in . . . what? not the movies, not that, but then what? a girl my age, pretty, but not sure of herself, attractive to men but not really liking herself all that much, and she drifts into one hurtful affair after another, and she's got some talent, sure, but there's something inside of her, some need she has that she doesn't want to admit to herself, the opposite of the wild side of the desperate hope and chance that brought her out here, because . . . because, even though it's a cliché, she had to admit it, she feels the biological clock ticking away in her, and she's not sure of either man, maybe, but she gets an abortion, because it's the business, she gives her whole life over to the business, and even though after a while things are going well, say, her mother calls and it all comes to her in the middle of the conversation just how sad she feels, you can see it on her face as she talks on the telephone, but then she tells herself it's okay, it's going to be all right, and maybe she can have both things, the work and a family when the right guy comes along, and she thought she found him in this young—what?—screenwriter? okay, okay, but I thought she wasn't going to be involved in the movies?—but say he is a screenwriter, or a lawyer, or what? say he runs a restaurant? no! or maybe a stable, yes, a riding stable just at the foot of the Santa Monicas, a surprising thing like that, something that most people not living out there would ever imagine, a stable in the middle of this huge city, and horses that travel in tunnels under the freeways, kicking up clouds of dust that rise into the air and fade into the smog, and say that they go out for a midnight ride, this woman and her friend, the man she loves, the man she adores, and it turns out that she's pregnant and doesn't even know it, maybe she's just missed a period and she's had some irregular periods in the past when she was under a lot of stress, and he tells her—what? that he's met someone else? or that he's gay? maybe that? which leads to the problem of the child and whether or not the man is infected, and say that the baby's going to be HIV? and they're going through hell because of it? and he decides to say the hell with it all? and takes off on his mount? his mount! and she races after him in the dark up the trail into the hills of garbage, calling out to him that she doesn't care, that she loves him no matter what? and in the dark she's galloping along—think of the scene, this scene, the dark trail, the city like an ocean all around this island made of trash—and the horse stumbles and throws her and the baby dies?

"Bee?"

A woman on horseback came trotting up out of the dark, calling my name as she rode.

"Hi," I said, giving the uncooperative Madonna another kick. But I still had trouble.

"You all right?" It was Balu Maginnes. "We thought you might have fallen."

"Where is everybody?" I said.

"Almost back at the stable by now, I'm sure," she said. "Roger sent me after you. I'm a better rider." She reached for my reins, but I pushed her hand aside.

"I'm okay," I said. "I've ridden before."

"So what were you doing up here?"

"Admiring the view," I said.

And then suddenly she turned her horse, and Madonna began to move and followed Balu's mount along the trail past the rest of the methane pumps and down along the sloping ridge and into the utter darkness of the steeply descending path. My cramps returned ten times worse than before. The trail went down and down, and I dared to turn in the saddle to try and ease my pain, and looked back up to where I had been lingering, dreaming all that time.

I could hardly breathe by the time we reached the stables, my nose and mouth and throat were so filled with dust, and my cramps had gotten even worse. Gary was standing there, his small hands planted on his slender hips, looking more miffed than worried. Bunny was waiting with him. So was Roger Maginnes. By the time I turned my horse over to the groom and got out of the bathroom in the stableman's office, Roger and Balu had gone.

"They said they had an early call," Gary said. "But I couldn't abandon you."

"Your legs are really going to hurt in the morning," Bunny said as she walked with us to the parking lot.

"And yours won't?" I said.

"It's just like fucking," she said. "You have to keep in shape."

Gary was staring at me. "Are you all right?" he said once we were inside the car.

"Yes, I'm fine."

I tried to sleep on the drive home, but the horse smell lay too thick on me, and I sat there, eyes closed, going over and over the treatment I had imagined in the dark. Once we got to the house, I asked Gary to feed the cat while I stripped off my clothes, tossed them into the washer, and took a hot soak. Bunny was right. My thighs throbbed in the stinging water.

After that, I lay in bed with Meow curled up into a purring ball near my head and the stuffed lamb I had bought at the mall tucked against my rumbling stomach. Next thing I knew, Gary was in the room, saying, "Telephone."

"Oh," I said, picking up the receiver.

"I woke you, didn't I?" Milt said in his nasal way.

"That's all right."

"I would have left a message on your machine, but I hate those things. I just wanted to say thanks in person. So . . . thanks."

"You're welcome," I said.

"I'm vell-come," he said.

"You are," I said. I looked up at Gary, who shrugged and left the room.

"Am I vell-come enough to maybe take you to dinner tomorrow night?" Milt said.

"You don't owe me anything for what I did," I said.

"I wasn't thinking about it like that," he said. "Nobody owes anybody anything. This would just be a dinner-dinner. So?"

"Can I think about it?"

"Okay," Milt said, and I was sorry to hurt his feelings. But I was too tired to explain anything anymore that night. Though after I hung up, I lay there a while listening to Meow's breathing and the distant hum of the spin cycle on the washer.

I was still awake when the next call came.

"Hello?"

"I told you we could talk."

"Roger," I said, "it's so late."

"I do some of my best business this time of night," he said.

Man in a Barrel

The skin beneath my fingernails splits painfully in winter, not the best thing in the world for a man who works with his hands. I've tried various kinds of lotions made from the stuff used by Norwegian fishermen, those poor bastards who spend cold years out on the water—I heard about the stuff on Paul Harvey—also secret formulas my ex-wife recommended and some of the medicines that the doctor I go to for my problem would suggest. Nothing does much good except a change in the weather, which wasn't on the horizon the morning I banged my pitiful thumb on the door handle as I tried to get my three boys into the Galaxie before all of us froze in that Albany wind.

"Last one in is a—" Tommy, my towheaded six-year-old, shouted a curse against his twin brothers as he claimed the front seat.

"And you're one too!" brown-haired Richie and Robby shouted at him as they fought their way into the back seat, those two a crazy gift from God or whoever in what turned out to be the stinking last year of my fading marriage to Nancy.

I closed the door on them, feeling the stinging in my fingers like something that would never go away. We were lucky because it had been a nearly snowless winter, something like a miracle for this part of the state. But this wind made it cold enough, and I had tried to get the boys to hurry. If I looked up at the house—which I didn't do as a matter of honor—I knew I would see Nancy peeking out at us at the corner of the window, ready to come out and say what she was thinking, which was I'm sure something like, Get those little boys into the car before they freeze, you asshole!

That look in her eye! If I ever had the flicker of a hope we might get back together, that look killed it. I can already see it sometimes in Tommy's eyes when something he doesn't like is going on, and I was thinking to myself they are getting to be like her and it will happen more and more so I better get my ass over to Albany more often.

So I was glad to be here, piling the boys into the car when I could have been right this minute flying down to Cancún, with Marty, his girl Pammy who's the secretary from over in the union office, and her roommate, what's her name, anyway? Reena? Riva? some weird name—I can't remember her name, even, I'm so bad with names, and I was about to spend the week with her down in Mexico—God, I took one look at her and said I sure as hell will!—until Nancy called and said that if I wanted a week with the boys it had to be this week and that was it.

"You—goddamn it!" I said to her, "who the hell are you to—"

She hung up on me.

I called back, apologizing, feeling those painful splits on my fingers and thumb.

"Look, okay, but I had other plans—"

"We have a life here," she said. "Next week, or I don't know when."

"Okay, okay," I said, thinking, there goes Cancún.

This turns out to be sort of all right, because when I told Marty that I wasn't going with him he says just as well since Pammy's roommate was getting cold feet anyway and it would have been a hell of a week if we got down there and it turned out she didn't want to play with me.

"Yeah, yeah," I said, running one of my stinging fingers around the rim of my glass, watching him light up yet another cigarette, something I gave up a while ago after the terrible pneumonia when Nancy and I were still together and the twins had just been born, and she looked over at me and said, "Honest to God, Jackson, we don't want to lose you; would you please give up those lousy cancer sticks!"

This gives me a little chill, and I'm thinking, Jesus, I can't even have a drink with my friend Marty at the Impala Grill across from the plant entrance without getting all moony inside about the old days with Nancy! even the bad old days toward the end!

Which led me to get up and leave much earlier than I would have usually, not having given up drinking, just the cigarettes, and I walked across the street to the parking lot where I stumbled around for a few minutes looking for my car.

Christ, I never pay attention to the numbers on the stanchions! I always tell myself I should write them down each day but I don't so I'm always staggering around this huge lot like one of those zombies out of *The Night of the Living Dead* we saw at Halloween over at what's-his-name's house, the sportswriter from the *News*. And then I saw this cute little blonde about four rows away, beating with her fists on the roof of a car.

"You know what your problem is?" I said to her when I got close enough to see the cause of her distress.

"What?" She turned around and looked at me like I was approaching her at midnight downtown instead of on a Tuesday at four o'clock with still a little sun shining through the mid-December clouds. "I can see what my problem is." She turned her face away.

"You're driving a Mazda," I said. "That's your problem. There are some guys on the line that ain't too happy about noticing a Japanese product on the property—or even in the state or the whole country, you know?"

"Creeps," she said, looking as though she was about to cry. "I only have one spare."

"Jesus, all four tires!" I said.

Well, it took a while, but I got her squared away, taking her in my car and helping her buy new tires and putting them on for her. This was a lot of time we spent together and she did some talking, about how she was a graduate student in psychology from Ann Arbor and she came to the plant to give out some questionnaires for a thing she was writing about guys on the line—and long before the end of it I'm wondering about getting together for a drink.

"Next week I go to New York state and bring my little boys back with me before Christmas," I said. "Who knows, sometime they might even come and live with me again."

"How many kids do you have?" she asked.

I held up three dirty fingers stinging like hell.

"That's a lot."

I nodded.

"Enough. Plenty."

"Well," she said.

"So you give me your number, maybe I'll call you after they go back?"

"Sure," she said. "That's kind of nice. How long you have them for?"

"Supposed to be a week," I said. "But it could be longer."

"Is that right?"

"They're mine as well as hers," I said. "You have any kids yourself?"

"Kids, no, I'm not even married. But . . . I have cats."

"Cats," I said.

"Cats."

"So," I said, and took her number and watched her drive away on her new radials. Susan Chapel, I think her name is; I almost forgot it, and I think to myself, hey, dummy, go write it down.

"DADDY?"

"Yo?" I said, and got sucked in to the fights going on in the back seat between the twins—Tommy, up front with me, is slumped over, asleep, his golden head pressed against the door, which I check, to be sure it's locked. Past Utica—and heading toward Syracuse. I break up the fight; another one flares up before we reach Syracuse.

"God damn it!" I reached around to slap whoever I could, feeling the car swerve, trying to hold my temper, and to keep my eye on the road. Jesus

Crow, I can hear Nancy's voice in my head telling me to drive carefully; do I want to kill them all?

Maybe I do, you bitch!

I can hear the echo of my own voice toward the end of things, Nancy shouting back at me, the boys crying, everything slipping down around my ankles and the water rising, all because I went out and did something stupid with a little Polack typist from over in personnel.

Hey, look, I said, maybe where you grew up nobody ever made mistakes, but where we lived, it just never was all that smart. I'm sorry, Nancy, okay? It will never happen again, I swear.

So we tried. But it was never the same for her. I can understand that now, looking at the snow starting to fall on us, past Syracuse, all three boys sleeping now, the tires humming that steady tune, like a straight line of sound all we had to do was follow and it would take us where we wanted to go.

A year after I had that fling Nancy left with the boys for Troy where she grew up, and then she took a place in Albany and started at nursing school, which is where I come in, I mean, which is where I come in as the visitor to my boys, driving over now and then to see them, taking the turnpike through Cleveland, then through Buffalo and along the Thruway to Albany, about a ten, twelve hour trip, depending on the time of day or night you drive it, the way you drive.

Nancy shared child-care with a bunch of other women at the school, which meant that she had to plan real carefully about her time, though none of this mattered to me much for a year or two after we split up. I was busy working a lot of overtime and when I wasn't working diddling around with that Polack girl again, and then some others, the kind of thing you always hear about happening after a guy like me who married young leaves his wife, or she leaves him, and it was one of those people, an Italian girl from Port Huron I met at a party, gave me this thing that acts up now and then.

You got cats? I got herpes, I should have said to the girl when I was putting on her new tires.

And then what could I tell her? Like everything else you read about in *Time* magazine, it's not as bad or as good as they make it out to be?

The doctor I went to for treatment was the one who gave me the idea about seeing the boys more often.

Sandy hair, a lot thinner than mine, wire-rim glasses, a Jewish guy by his name, but he didn't look Jewish.

"This is the kind of thing that gets worse because of stress," he told me.

"Stress?" I said.

"That's right. You'll suffer less of a reaction if you find ways to reduce your stress. I'm going to give you some medication, too, but the best thing that can help you is—"

"Get rid of my stress," I finished for him.

Try saying that to yourself in the machine shop at Ford's, I wanted to put in. But we had started talking about ways I could do that, and the kids came up, and he suggested that if I saw them more often, I would worry less about my life, drink less, smoke less.

"Sting less?" I put in.

"That stuff with your fingers, you ought to see a dermatologist about that," he said. "It could be some sort of fungus."

"Not stress?"

"It could be stress related, sure."

"Stress, stress, everything is stress. I know about stress, I work with metal, you know? But I'm not made of steel."

"That's exactly my point," the doctor said. "You need to relax a little."

"That's what got me in here in the first place," I said.

He laughed.

"Sorry," he said. "But you really ought to think about taking some time off. Take a little vacation. Take your kids somewhere."

I nodded, wondering just where I could take them. But other things came to mind real quick.

"I ought to kill that girl," I said.

"Don't do that," he said. "You wouldn't like it in prison."

"No, no," I said, shaking my head, "I wouldn't."

I did try to find her, though, to tell her what happened to me, but like many girls she had only roommates, no family, and all they told me when I called was that she had moved.

"Good thing," Marty said when I told him, "or else you might have killed the bitch."

"Naw," I said, shaking my head, drinking my fourth or fifth beer.

"Look," he said, "just listen to the doctor. It couldn't hurt you to go somewhere with the kids. You're lucky to get next to them. Mine don't talk to me anymore."

"Any more advice?" I said.

He smiled slyly at me. "Yeah, next time you're out on a date? Wear a condom."

"Yeah, hey, thanks, Dr. Ruth," I said, getting up from the bar and going to where I lived. I can't call it home. We had a little house but when we split up we sold it and Nancy put the money toward her nursing school tuition. So I lived in an apartment, one bedroom, kitchen, a little living room, on the second floor of a building maybe a mile or two from where I grew up. If my folks were still alive, I would probably have gone to their house for supper. As it was, I picked up a pizza and went to my place and washed it down with a beer.

And then a couple more.

"Hey, pal, listen up!" Marty called me from the Impala a little later.

"To what?"

Then he told me the details of the trip to Cancún he had just arranged after his Pammy and her friend whatever her name is came in to the bar.

"See, it's all working out," he said.

"I was thinking of taking my kids somewhere sometime," I said.

"Pammy's friend is almost young enough to be your daughter. Does that help?"

"Fuck you," I said.

"No, fuck her," he said. "And listen, talking about age, you need your birth certificate, don't forget," he said.

"Why, am I getting married again?"

"For Mexico. You got to write for it quick."

"I keep all those things around," I said. "Since the divorce, I keep all that stuff in a metal box right here."

"Good for you," he said.

"Yeah, good for me," I said.

And so after we finished talking I went over to the dresser and dug around for the divorce papers, because I knew my birth certificate should be there, too.

And then I found out from Nancy that she wanted me to pick up the boys for this week before Christmas and so I took some vacation time, and so that's how—the short version—I'm driving along, thinking about all this, and I really got to laugh at myself, the way I've made a mess of things.

Cats?

No, herpes.

My life hadn't always been this way, I was thinking as the boys began to make waking noises. I was once their age, small as them, full of piss and vinegar, my folks still alive, dreaming of saving up a ton of cash and leaving the country, going to work as a machinist in South America or somewhere, I don't know what I was thinking. I shook my head, stared at the road signs. *Batavia*, a sign said. Sunlight broke through the clouds, stayed a little while, then faded. The boys were mixing it up again in the back seat.

"You want me to go over the fucking edge?" I shouted at them. "You want that?"

All three boys started crying at once, and I reached around and tried to pat the twins and then Tommy, who was sitting as close to the door as he could.

"All right, all right, boys," I said. Another sign flashed past. "Hey, did you see that?" Tommy looked out the window. I couldn't see what the twins were doing. "Hey, see that? *Niagara Falls!* Hey, boys, what if we cross over into Canada and take a look at the greatest sight you ever saw!"

They started squealing and asking question after question—and so the noise continued while I was concentrating on my plan, which was instead of swinging west toward Cleveland at Buffalo we'd take the bridge over to Canada, drive the twenty or so miles to the falls, and then see what we could see. We could make the rest of the trip through Ontario on the Canadian side of Lake Erie and cross back into Detroit from Windsor. Who knows what could happen? I was asking myself as we took the cutoff for the International Bridge, bouncing along that bad stretch of road.

"Hey, Tommy, look at those potholes," I said, wondering why I say these things to my boys. There are plenty of other things I could say, but I say, look at the potholes.

"What?" Tommy said.

"What? what?" the twins piped up from the back seat.

I'm thinking—how do you account for such things?—I'm thinking, I'll call that girl when I get back, soon as I get back, Susan Chapel (?) . . .

The toll booth . . . the bridge.

"Over to Canada now boys," I said.

"Does Mom know we're going?" Tommy seemed a little nervous as we crossed over the rough waters where Lake Erie narrows and flows north toward the falls and Lake Ontario.

"No, why should she?"

I was staring down at the water, wondering why it wasn't running even faster than it was, but it was running, I'll tell you.

"I don't want Conneckutt," one of the twins said.

"What?" I said.

"I don't want to be in Conneckutt," he said.

"Hey, you're in Canada," I said as we rolled off the bridge onto the roadway and slowed down at the immigration booths. This sour-faced young guy in uniform leaned out of the booth for a look inside into the car.

FIVE MINUTES LATER and we've turned around and we're heading right back across the bridge, the boys crying, and my heart all full of rage. How did I know I needed to have a notarized letter from Nancy saying that I could take the kids into Canada?

"I just want to show the boys the falls," I told the guy.

"Take them to the American side, sir," he said.

"Well, fuck you, I will," I said.

He stared down at me, like he was waiting for something.

"Sorry about that," I said. "How do I get there?"

He gave me directions and in front of all the other cars I had to make a U-turn and head back to the U.S. side.

"You're lucky, after all, Robbie," I said, "we're not going to Conneckutt."

"Yeah," he said through his tears.

"We're not?" his brother said.

"Nope," I said, "we're staying in the good old U.S. of A."

"Daddy?" Tommy said.

"Yep?"

"I got to pee."

"We'll do that," I said, "and then I'm going to show you the greatest sight you've ever seen in your life!"

"Good morning," the uniformed girl in the American booth said.

"Good morning," I said, looking up at her, and seeing a little resemblance to the woman with the cats. Just a little.

"Where are you headed?" She leaned down and looked at Tommy and then at the twins.

I explained how we were trying to get to the falls and that they turned us around at the Canadian side.

"You're U.S. citizens?"

"They don't make 'em more American than we are," I said.

She paused a moment, and then smiled and said, "Our side's just as pretty. It's just not as built up."

"Point me in the right direction," I said.

And that's how after we stopped so I could take the kids into the bathroom and I bought them some burgers at a fast-food place, we came to be driving along on the American side of the widening strip of water running out of Lake Erie. Along the shore I noticed the water didn't seem to be running that fast, though I knew it had to be moving pretty quick, like all of us, the river, the kids, me, rushing along toward whatever it was we had started out to meet a long time ago when we began our trip.

And then I saw that tower of mist rising along the shore, and I told the kids to look and at first they couldn't see it, and then they did, and to me it looked like pictures of a whale spouting, or some geyser, Old Faithful, shooting into the air, nothing that I'd ever seen in person, only in pictures or in the movies.

"Thar she blows!" I shouted.

And the boys echoed that all the way along the road that parallels the river, where the water really picks up momentum, heading directly toward the place where that mist was rising and I had to flick on the wipers and I knew that we were really in for something.

"Daddy," Tommy said, noticing that big umbrella of mist.

The twins kept quiet, an amazing thing since they weren't asleep.

We pulled into a parking lot and I got the boys out of the car, turned their collars up, buttoned their coats—my fingers stinging—and herded them along toward the railing. A few people stood around, pointing, staring out into the mist and the rumbling, roaring falls. And I was saying to the boys, "You know, guys, this goes on every second, winter, summer, spring," and I was saying to myself, this rumbling, the rising mist, amazing. Weather changes, but this thing goes on forever, though I had a vague memory of hearing somewhere on some TV news program that the water was wearing down the rocks and that in a million years or so the falls would be sort of smoothed out.

"Wow," Tommy was saying, over and over.

The twins still kept their mouths shut, following along behind their older brother as I led them all to the place at the railing where we looked down at the thundering rush of river tumbling over the edge of the falls into the hugest boiling pit of water I'd ever seen, like it was God took the

river and broke it over his knee and forever after the water fell all this distance. The sound—the sound was like a freight train running right past
you all the time.

So I had to raise my voice to speak to the boys—all three of them a
little stunned by the sight of this thing—all the noise, the space, the rising
geyser of mist, the rushing breadth of the towering falls of water so white it
might have been a hole poked through to another kind of place— "Guys,"
I said. "Guys, pay attention! Every day, while you guys are playing or going
to the bathroom or eating macaroni and cheese or brushing your teeth, this
water here is falling just like this . . . I want you to take a good look, because
I want you to remember it, understand?" Tommy nodded, but the twins
were ignoring me, hypnotized by the sight. "You hear me?"

So this is why we came here, I said to myself. I didn't really want to
admit what I was doing, taking the kids like this and trying to cross over into
Canada, but here we were on the American side and it was all right, *this* was
why I had come, to point out this wonder to them, to say the words to them
that I had just said.

And that was when Tommy shouted, "Look!"

And I noticed the young Indian couple, at least I thought to myself
Indian, though they could have been Pakistani or some other kind of
people from that part of the world.

Tommy meant for me to see that the man was wearing a turban; I
figured that out later. I noticed the funny thing going on between the man
and the woman as they walked just ahead of us along the railing. The noise
of the falls was so loud I couldn't hear them, but I could see them talking
and sort of passing the bundle—it was a baby, Tommy said, no, it's a doll,
he said after he looked again—back and forth.

You take this, they went.

No, you take this.

No, you take it.

No, you carry it.

No, you.

There were other people passing by, fathers and mothers with children tagging along just like the twins were, and Tommy, and I was thinking how I never took Nancy here, and what if I had? and what if I brought that woman Susan Chapel (?), and I was already planning to ask Marty and Pammy if they wanted to take the trip, just overnight, but they had to see this thing, this great wonder is what I have to call it, and that was when Richie asked me to tie his shoelace, and Robby said that his was untied too, and so I stopped and bent down—all the time the mist is falling on us like light rain—and when I finished and stood up the Indian man was running toward the parking lot while the woman stood just in front of us screaming, pointing into the mist.

I shouted at Tommy to stay with the boys—hold their hands!—and took off after the turban into the parking lot. He was crying and running, almost loping along like a gut-shot deer, and you could tell he was in trouble even if you hadn't seen what he had just done.

"You—hey!" I called after him, feeling the hot air in my lungs, so different from the cold mist on my face and neck.

He turned, looking over his shoulder, stunned, like I had just called him a dirty name, singling him out of a crowd of innocent bystanders—and then kept on running.

I caught up with him right at the lip of the parking lot, grabbing him by the coat and swinging him around, slamming my fist into his face.

Jeez, it wrecked my hand!

But I hit him again, and then again, noticing but not caring that the blood on his cheeks was glistening almost like it was some kind of oil I was rubbing into the mahogany of his skin.

A cop pulled me off the guy, and I was shaking like crazy, and it felt like I might have broken one of the little bones in my hand.

"We got him now, sir," the cop said, pushing the Indian guy to the ground.

"Did you save the kid?" I asked the cop, as I stared down at the Indian guy and saw that he was shivering the same way I was shivering.

"We got our people out there, sir," the cop said, one hand on top of the Indian guy's turban, like this man was some kind of Jack in the Box he was holding down. "You saw him throw the baby over?"

"I don't just go around punching out strangers for the hell of it," I said.

Tommy came up, one twin on each hand.

"I saw you hit him, Daddy."

"What else did you see, sonny?" the cop said.

"That man threw his baby into the water," Tommy said.

Another cop came over and they talked and then the first one said they wanted me to come to the station to make a statement. I looked over at the Indian guy and he looked up at me and it was so crazy because just then he nodded at me, nodded, like he was saying, Don't worry, it's okay, or, Right, we did what we had to do, or, We did a good job together, right?

BY THE TIME we got through with all this it was too late to keep on driving. At the station, they gave me the name of a motel, which was where the kids and I ended up staying the night.

I fed the boys at the motel restaurant and then read them a story—I don't remember what that story was now—and put them to bed.

"I don't like Conneckutt," Richie said.

"Me, neither," his brother said.

"Daddy?" Tommy said from the other bed where he would bunk with me.

"Yeah?"

"Did they find the baby?"

"Jeeezus Icehouse," I said, "are you kidding?"

But then I was sorry because he began to cry and I told him some stuff about the way the cops went out in the police boat and how they might just find it. That seemed to calm him, though whether he believed it or not I couldn't say for sure.

After the boys fell asleep I walked around the room, turned on the bathroom light and left the door open a crack, and then went downstairs to the bar where I had a few beers, enough to get me to take a little stroll outside. I got as far as the parking lot and there I stood, listening to that roar, thinking how these goddamn falls pour down their millions and millions of gallons every hour, every day, every month, every year, and would for a million years, on and down and on. Tomorrow boats would go out again into those waters, looking for a dead Indian baby.

What kind of a man would do that to his own child? I asked myself. What kind of a man would do that to any child?

The frightened bloodied face of the man in the turban floated up in front of me, but I pushed it away.

My hand was aching and the wind stung my eyes and drove me back inside. I went upstairs and rearranged the covers on the trio of boys. I sat for a little bit in front of the telephone, just sort of nodding off from the beer, then coming to with a start, taking a look at myself in the mirror in front of me. After a while I picked up the telephone and, nursing my fingers, dialed the number.

It rang and rang, but just as I was giving it up her voice came on the line.

"Hello?" I said in a whisper.

"Yes?"

"Is this Susan . . . Chapel? Keeper of cats?"

"Who is this?"

So filled with hope, I lied and lied and lied.

The Tunnel

One week after their candidate lost the election Jas and her roommate Sharon were getting ready for a party, Jas stepping into her flashiest skirt, the silver-sequined wraparound, and wondering about a blouse. She was a tall girl, so skirts like this looked good on her. She had narrow hips, long legs—good, firm breasts, that was true, and a long neck. My swan, her dad used to tease her, lovingly. My swan. Who wanted to be a swan? Swans were oddly beautiful, but were they happy? That was the question that bothered Jas whenever she recalled her father's pet name for her.

When she thought of her mother, it was another sort of memory, much more deeply tinged with emotion. Her mother had told her nearly every day of her life that her eyes were beautiful, and Jas felt her chest constrict—and seem to turn to ice at the same time—at the picture in her mind of her mother, just before she went into that last surgery, unable to speak but blinking hard at her, blinking, blinking, which meant, your eyes, your eyes. All she needed was to have a boy look her in the eyes and he'd be a goner. That was her mother's constant refrain. But so far no one tall enough to look properly into her eyes—and there had only been a few of those anyway—was anyone she wanted to look back at. There had been one or two guys at school whom she had gone out with more than once, but nothing happened with them. All they wanted was sex, and she just couldn't, not yet, not so soon, she told herself, after her mother's death. There had been no one in the year after graduation when she had worked in downtown Detroit. No one these last six months when she had worked on the Committee to Re-Elect the President, first in Michigan and then—because of a little fling Sharon had had with a committee man passing through the state, a two-night stand, actually—here in Washington.

"Fletcher said it's going to be a great party, even if we did lose," her roommate said, stepping up next to her in front of the mirror.

Jas gave her a queer look.

"You didn't ask him to bring a friend for me, did you?"

"No." Sharon looked at her in the mirror looking at her.

"Look me in the eye and say that," Jas said, turning to Sharon and touching a hand to her friend's shoulder.

"I'll call a taxi for us," Sharon said, moving toward the telephone.

"I knew it!"

Jas stalked past her, went to the window, pretended to study the dark street below.

In the taxi, Jas enjoyed seeing the wide marble buildings lining the wide avenue, and as they approached Georgetown, the narrow but stately colonial brick houses with an occasional wood-frame mansion between. Up toward Dumbarton Oaks the vehicle carried them, the driver listening intently to the scratchy radio calls in a language neither girl could put a name to.

"Good address," Sharon said when they pulled up in front of a three-story house with a wonderful white porch on R Street.

"Whose house again?" Jas had forgotten.

"Daughter of Senator Whoosis," Sharon said slyly as they stepped from the cab into a gutter full of crackling leaves.

"Republican or Democrat?" Jas said.

"What do you think?" Sharon said. "Democrats have all the good parties."

"To make a bad pun," Jas put in.

"Ouch," Sharon said. "But it's true. Fletcher knows her husband, a photographer. They met on some trek or other in the Himalayas."

"Tibet or not Tibet, that is the question."

Sharon gave her a playful shove as they climbed the steps to the front porch.

"You have a great sense of humor. And such great eyes."

"Thanks," Jas said, noticing heads bobbing past the large picture window. Through the glass panes in the door they could see a thick curtain of coats hung on hooks along the wall.

Sharon rang the bell. Jas felt a little jolt, the old pain in her chest. Ever since the end of sophomore year at college it had visited her regularly. Will I ever be happy the way other people seem to be happy? And then, as usual—fortunately—her mind danced away from the thought.

There was a lot to distract her once they went inside. Their hostess, a petite woman wearing a long black dress and a Tibetan necklace of some sort—Sharon asked, so they learned that it *was* from Tibet—introduced them to the nearest group of people: a broad-chested national correspondent for a chain of midwestern newspapers, his mousey wife, a weak-chinned professor of philosophy from Georgetown—maybe he'd been a priest once, Jas figured from the way he spoke and looked at her—and a sour-faced fellow who wrote a political column for one of the local newspapers, the one with the lowest circulation. None of the men came up to Jas's collarbone.

"I understand you're going to be out of a job," the philosophy professor said.

"That's right," Jas said. "We lost."

"Poignant," said the professor.

"Are you looking around?" said the wife of the national correspondent. "There's always something else to do in this town."

Before Jas could think of a response the circle of people shifted, and the national correspondent's wife led him across the room but not before Jas caught a whiff of his foul-smelling breath. A thick-necked, shifty-eyed bull of a man the color of maple syrup drifted past; people said hello, hello, and then he was gone to another room. Then Sharon appeared, accompanied by the tallest guy Jas had seen in town in the past six months of her stay.

"Jas, this is Charles. Charles, Jas."

"My name is actually Josephine," Jas said, "but nobody calls me that."

His eyes were level with hers and she stared a moment, watched him blink.

"Can I get you a drink?"

"Oh!" Jas laughed and swept her right arm out to the side, knocking someone's shoulder with her outstretched hand.

"Excuse me," she said as the man turned to stare at her with cold blue eyes, glaring at first and then smiling, his cheeks crinkling up in a charming way.

"Of course," he said and turned back to his conversation with the national correspondent and his wife.

"Easy on my boss," the tall guy said.

"That's your boss?"

"That's my Senator," he said. There was something about this young man's eyes Jas noticed now—they were red-rimmed, as though he lacked moisture for his contacts or had been up all night talking, and whatever else. "Something to drink?"

And she said, yes, fine, and he brought her a glass of wine and asked her questions about the office and commiserated with her about its imminent closing. He managed to ask if he could call her.

"May I?" he said, like some lanky little boy in grade school asking for permission for a bathroom pass.

HE CALLED A few days later, catching Jas and Sharon in the middle of clearing out their closets.

"Oh, my God," she heard herself say, trying to dig herself a little cave amidst the pile of sweaters and old running clothes. "I can't, I just can't."

"You mean you won't?" His voice sounded mournful at the other end of the line.

"I'm just so busy," she said. "We're closing our office, and I've got tons of work before I even start looking for another job."

"So you're going to stay in the city?"

"I don't know," Jas said, her voice turning a little childish. "I don't know."

"It's something to do," Sharon said after Jas had hung up.

"I am not going out with someone just because we are the same height."

"I know people who've gotten together for worse reasons," her room-mate said.

"Who?"

"Our parents."

"If he calls again, I'll see," Jas said, plucking at the collar of an old sweater from college with her sorority letters embroidered on the sleeve.

But she must have really put him off, she decided. Weeks went by, and they were nearly out of a job when Rosaliza, the secretary-receptionist in their soon-to-be-former office, suggested that Jas do a little research on government agencies where they all might look for something. That's what you were reduced to in this town if you worked for the party out of power and you had little experience and fewer contacts. So she found herself in the Library of Congress spending hours going over lists of possibilities. The high-ceilinged room where she sat suggested such promise, the gilt of its decorations, the names of the greats, that she worked on and on in the midst of many others, from the elderly with noses pressed to their books to girls new to college whose purposes would in a few years turn out, she guessed, to be similar to her own. Find a job, hope for love — oh, Jas, she chided herself, get on with the work and leave the daydreaming to those with the time to do it. She fingered the collar of her blouse while she read and made her notes, closing her eyes now and then and wondering, as a chill spread across her neck and down her spine, just what she was going to do with herself.

When she left the reading room and made her way to the elevators, the air around her chilled her and she pulled her coat close to her chest. A stout black guard watched as she stopped at the elevator door. She smiled at him. He looked the other way.

The car arrived and she stepped inside, pushing what she took to be the button for the ground floor. Alone in the descending car, she breathed hard and sighed, for what reason she could not figure, just the general sadness of it all, she supposed—from the loneliness of independence, of course, her father might say.

Down she went, down past the first floor and the ground floor. Oops! Wrong button after all! It would have been comical, she decided in that instant, typical of her life—if when the door opened she hadn't felt a sudden surge of fear. But there was only a cream-colored wall and a sign with an arrow pointing to the right. She shrugged and stepped out of the car and with some caution followed the arrow along a narrow corridor with peeling paint and peeling pipes overhead. Somehow the arrow gave her comfort.

An angular woman with skin the color of brown velvet appeared around the corner, an identity card dangling from her neck on a long metal chain.

"Is this the way out?" Jas said.

"Follow the signs." The woman looked her over and walked around her.

Jas marched forward, finding herself in a room with vending machines and the odor of coffee hanging in the air. A few young library workers— she noticed their identity cards—lounged about on plastic chairs, food scattered on tables before them, papers on the floor. A thick-necked boy with braids and a bright red comb jutting out from behind his ear stared up at her as she passed. He signaled to his companion, an older fellow wearing one of those hooded sweatshirts Jas had noticed were all the rage. She hurried from the room, finding herself in another curving passageway that led in two quick turns to a broad tunnel whirring with the hum of turbines and the echo of distant voices.

The tunnel was broad and wide—rectangular rather than tubular as she might have imagined it—and sloping slightly upward several hundred yards as though it were a roadway beneath a river and led to another shore. From that distance a gaggle of formidable women, their faces ranging in color from onyx to near-purple, charged toward her down the incline, laughing, waving hands at each other. The tallest was only three quarters of Jas's height, and they glanced up at her—the shortest of them openly stared—as they passed her by.

Jas quickened her stride, passing doors on either side marked PERSONNEL ONLY and EMERGENCY ONLY. Within a few minutes she had walked halfway to the other end. The exit to the street had to be somewhere off in the distance where a group of men in suits now turned the corner and came walking swiftly toward her down the incline. As they approached—five of them, all of them fairly tall and most of them with a full head of hair—Jas instinctively glanced down at her breasts, and then, fixing a serious expression on her face, straightened up and kept walking forward.

"Hey," the tallest of them said from a distance of about thirty feet or so. The man nearest him used his elbow on the tall one while the others stared at her. "Hello," she said as they passed.

"Just a minute," the tall one said to the others, another of whom, the man in the center, she recognized by his cold blue stare: the Senator.

"Hey," the tall guy—it was Charles— slowed down and tilted his head to one side.

"Hey," Jas said, stopping to speak.

"You never called me back," Charles said.

"I didn't?"

"Nope."

"You never called me again," Jas said.

"I will now," he said, giving her a little wave and then making clear with his hands that he had to hurry after the others. "Ceremony over at the Adams building. Got to go."

"B-bye," Jas said, watching for a moment as he rushed along the wide corridor to catch up with his group. Then she was moving again, her mind full of new questions, stopping only when startled by a dark-headed young black man who stepped sideways out of one of the side doors.

"Excuse me," she said, afraid she'd made some sound of distress. The young man kept on walking ahead of her as though she were not there. On the street, at night, say, this might have seemed sinister. In the brightly lighted tunnel, Jas thought nothing of it. The black man stopped at the elevator. When she came near she noticed that despite his wiry build the top of his head was barely level with her shoulder. The elevator door slid open, he stepped inside, and she followed. She said a hello and only then did he look at her, his eyes full of veins and flecks. He wore a brown cardigan nearly the color of his flesh and a pair of neatly creased brown trousers. His two smooth cheeks gave off an appealing odor of a familiar aftershave, the name of which she could not recall. Almost as if he could read her mind, the man raised a hand and touched a finger to his cheek—all this in what seemed like absolute slow-motion—revealing a gold band on an appropriate finger.

"Floor?" the man said, his voice high-pitched and almost boyish.

Before Jas could answer they both turned at the sound of running feet and saw Charles charging up to the car.

"Whoa!" he said and leaped inside. "Nearly missed you!" He pressed a button. The other man pressed another button. The car gave a shudder as the doors closed and it began to rise.

"What are you doing?" Jas said, eyebrows raised, her hands balled nervously into fists at her sides.

"Coming after you," he said.

The other man threw her a furtive look, then glanced at Charles.

"You okay?" the man said to Jas.

"She's okay," Charles said.

The black man shrugged as the elevator car jerked to a halt and the doors slid open. He took one more look at her and stepped out of the car.

"Thank you," she said.

"I have a proposition for you," Charles said as he moved along with Jas out of the car.

"What?"

"Don't get worried. This is business. Come with me and listen to what I have to say."

So they left the Library and walked back along the street toward the Senate Office Building. It was one of those days near winter when the sun beat brightly down and there was little wind. Jas felt warm enough to open her coat and she swung her arms freely as she walked and listened to Charles's proposal.

"The Senator wants me to work for him?" she said when he had finished. "He doesn't even know who I am."

"In fact, he does," Charles said, moving his arms in wide arcs as he explained.

"Sharon sent over our resumes?"

"Uh-huh."

"And he wants to hire her, too?"

"If she's willing."

"So this is how it's done?" Jas shook her head. Standing at the curb before the Supreme Court Building waiting for the cars to pass, the Capitol dome glowing in the sun at a distance across the street, she felt as though she were waiting in a dream—the marble buildings all around her, the bare tree branches overhead, the sun splashed across the white-pale sky.

She returned to the apartment so full of news she could scarcely speak. Sharon had the same look in her eye, the same trembling in her lips and hands.

"You got two job offers!" Jas couldn't believe the coincidence. It was like living in a story, it was like a soap opera. Except that this was her life — their real lives.

"I write a great letter, let's face it," her roommate said. "Fletcher helped, of course. He's got the knack. So what about Charles? Do you think he has it too?"

Jas could feel the heat of a blush rising to her cheeks, but she talked right through the sensation.

"If he's not just bullshitting, it's a good job. You ought to think about coming with me. I—"

"Fletcher thinks the Education Association is a good entry for me," Sharon said.

Jas cared about Sharon, so she backed away from the subject.

"So you think I should take this job?" Jas asked.

"I think you should jump at it."

She jumped. She went to the office and filled out the forms. She met the staff. She endured the obligatory interview with the Senator himself, who fixed her with those stone-blue eyes for about twelve seconds before nodding and offering a soft hand and saying, "Welcome aboard."

"When do you begin?" her father asked her when she went home for Christmas. His eyes seemed different from the way she remembered them—soft, glassy, threads of red running out from the dark pupils.

"Soon as I get back," she told him.

"I was worried when the campaign committee shut down," he said. "I didn't know what you were going to do."

"It's a big town, Papa," she said, "with a lot of opportunities."

"I worry about some of those opportunities," he said. "I sit at home and worry quite a bit about some of those opportunities."

It went like that for a couple of days more, whether they were sitting in the old renovated train station turned restaurant watching the snow fall onto the rarely used tracks, or in the living room watching McNeil-Lehrer before she cooked his favorite meal, or in the car to the airport.

"Say hello to the President for me," he said.

She laughed. "At least I'll say hello to the Senator."

"Just be careful," he said. She could still hear his sorrowful voice as the airplane tilted its nose into the snow and edged upward toward the clouds.

Back in her empty apartment Jas found sleeping difficult with Sharon still away at her parents' house. The apartment became a theater of suspicious noises, threatening sounds. The next day when Sharon returned they killed two bottles of wine as they sat up late, talking, drinking; the warm glow seemed to soften Jas's holiday blues.

New Year's Eve: the two of them back at the house of the daughter of Senator Whoosis. Jas had never met her hostess the first time; now she spent the first few minutes discussing the city's winter weather with her. Her husband, the photographer, wasn't at home, she learned. He was somewhere in Tibet, chasing some elusive mountain goat with his camera. The Senator stood on the other side of the room, his wife in tow, a doll-like woman with bright made-up eyes, a slash of crimson across the place where her mouth would be. Even at this distance Jas had to look away from his stare. She was relieved to see the burly foul-breathed national correspondent and his wife, and the sour-faced philosophy professor, and the political columnist.

"Hi," she said, and they made polite noises and asked her questions. They all seemed to know about her new job. She spoke, her mind replaying the events of the past year—that's what this time of the night did for her, especially after she'd had a few glasses of wine—the dissolving of her old job, the meeting with Charles in the tunnel—but where was he tonight? Not that she cared. She looked around. Somehow midnight had crept up on them and music filled the room. Sharon was dancing with a pink-faced stranger in a beautiful blue jacket. Jas's mood picked up. She shuffled her feet in place to the music.

Next morning, her stomach gurgling, her eyes filmed over with cataract-like veils, she yanked herself out of bed and went stumbling toward the bathroom only to find Sharon's dance partner sitting on the toilet. She backed out of the bathroom and stood at the window of the living room. Two men in hooded sweatshirts came loping along the street, tapping on car hoods as though they were steel drums. Jas crawled back into bed and stayed awhile.

That New Year's Day, a day full of physical discomfort and the resumption of the winter blues, led off a raw January, a month when Jas spent little time outdoors. She was having doubts about her political beliefs, and it

wasn't a great time for someone who had worked to reelect the ousted President to stroll about the streets. Either she holed up in her new cubicle at
the Senate Office Building or—the week of the inaugural, when she was
hit with a terrible cold—she burrowed into her bed at home with reports
to read, and now and then a novel to clear her mind. She read about the
environmental impact of coal processing plants in her Senator's home
state, and she read about an honest young lawyer chased through the
streets of Memphis on the run from killer partners. Neither was entirely
real; neither was at all satisfying.

Sometimes, though, she and Sharon—just as alone now, it seemed, as
she was—had a good laugh together, and now and then they went out to
the Hawk and Dove. Late nights, all smoke and beery air, it seemed jovial
enough at first. Eyes meeting glances of men at the bar, men Jas recognized from the corridors of the office building, other men strangers with a
familiar look, thin steel-rimmed glasses, ties askew, dark hair slicked back
with either water or pomade. They glanced at her, she glanced back, then
looked away. The end of a basketball game on the television screen
mounted above the bar. Black men, much taller than she, galloping along
the court in one direction and then turning on a dime and galloping back
again.

Hurrying home through the dark and chill, Sharon jabbering away
about something, how one of the guys at the bar had said something to her,
Jas wondering about the street ahead, the dark, the cold days to come.
Soon it would get lighter earlier, stay light longer. Something to look forward to. Shoes squeaking on the pavement. The sound of their voices, their
breathing. At the corner a taxi dropped some people at the hotel. Jas and
Sharon crossed the street. Suddenly out of an alley shot a man on a bike.
He wheeled around in front of them, a wide-faced man, his eyes lost in the
darkness of his hooded sweatshirt.

"Girls," he said.

"Let's go," Sharon said, and Jas nearly tripped as they made a wide
berth around him, fast-walking in the street for the next half block.

"Ladies," the rider said, coming up behind them.

"Go away," Jas said as she broke into a trot.

"Wait for me," Sharon said, hurrying along behind.

Rushing to their building, rushing up the steps. Jas at the top of the stoop dared to look back and saw an empty street.

"The phantom rider," Jas said.

"Don't even joke," Sharon said. "I hate this."

"My father has a word for it," Jas said as she let them inside. "Modern girls in the modern world. He calls the dangers we worry about 'opportunities.'"

"Very funny," Sharon said.

"He lost his sense of humor when my mother died," Jas said.

A week later Sharon came into her room late at night and sat down on the edge of the bed.

"Fletcher ask you to marry him?"

"Not exactly," she said. "But I'm moving in with him."

Jas switched on the bedlamp and grabbed her friend's hands.

"I'm so happy for you!"

"I feel like a shit," Sharon said.

"I won't say a word about the guy who stayed over."

Sharon shook her head.

"Not about that, dummy," she said. "About you. About abandoning you."

"You're not," Jas said, feeling herself sink into the bed.

"I just can't live here anymore," Sharon said. "It makes me too nervous. I know I'm being a coward . . ."

"You're not," Jas said again, something shifting in her chest as Sharon went on with her explanation.

A week later and she found herself alone in the apartment, with no immediate financial need for a new roommate since Sharon, in her guilt, had written her a check—God knows where she got the money, maybe borrowed it from home—for half of the next three months' rent. But Jas had other worries. The night noises of the building kept her constantly in a state of nerves. Walking home alone, she focused on her demeanor, walked in a way that she took to be determined, street-wise, like someone with a mission, not one of those day-or-night dreamers who get knocked off by roving muggers. Sharon called her often those first few weeks, and they talked a lot, almost as much as when they lived together. Jas watched television for company, silly shallow TV movies that made her sniffle, sometimes even weep at the most ludicrous and artificial circumstances. With respect to her own circumstances, she kept herself tough, only now and then indulging herself with chocolate and an occasional call to her father.

"You're alone?" he asked the first time they talked after Sharon's departure.

"Don't sound so worried. I'm a big girl and it's a safe building."

"That's not what I was thinking."

"What then, Pa?"

"I know all about being alone. Take care of yourself, please, would you?"

She wasn't sure how she was supposed to do that. But just after the first day of spring when Charles came up to her desk out of the blue and leaned over and asked if she wanted to go out for a beer she said okay.

He was company, and not bad company at that. Over their beers at the Hawk and Dove he had stories to tell about the office, the Senator, about a number of odd and amusing occurrences among the denizens of the same halls they walked each day. A trivial thought, she knew, but she didn't even have to lean over when they talked. At eye-level with Charles she felt more relaxed than with most people toward whom she had to stoop. Wandering back along Pennsylvania Avenue, she felt safer than she had in months. Even when they walked past the entrance to the Capitol Hill Suites where she saw a hooded bike rider flash past in the dim glow of the street lamp she felt secure, pointing him out to Charles, though the rider disappeared around the corner before she could explain. Charles kept close to her, and she bumped hips with him once or twice as they walked.

And talked about the new President.

"A bum," Charles said. "Runs well, but if these first few months are indicative, he sure as hell doesn't know how to govern."

"But he's smart, don't you think?" Jas said, tasting beer on her words.

"Yeah, sure," Charles said. "But that's not always a good thing to be in this town. Most of the elected officials are just average brains. They don't like it when anybody stands out too much above them. It's like . . . being our height, you know what I mean?"

"I guess I do," Jas said.

They had reached Jas's block and she slowed down, holding to Charles's arm, and settled into a stroll, as though it were full-blown spring out here and light, maybe eleven in the morning or three in the afternoon.

"Nice night," Charles said.

"Thank you," Jas said, stopping them as they reached her building.

"Home?" he said. "Nice building." He kept his eyes on her.

"Come up?" she said. "How about some coffee?"

Upstairs she pointed him toward the sofa while she went to the stove. Standing there she felt the oddest sensation, not a palpable feeling but more a sense of absence, as though she had left her body and floated above the burners, light and airy and buoyant, yet anchored somehow to the floor so that she could not float away. She touched the coffeepot. She touched the switch for the gas. She touched a finger to her collarbone, traced it, pushed, probed. Next thing she knew he was standing next to her.

"Maybe I'll have a beer instead," he said.

"In the fridge," she said, holding to the stove.

A few minutes later she tried to stand, only to fall back onto the sofa where he had led her with an easy looseness of bones and muscles. She stood again—the room must have moved—and then fell back—onto the bed. Her sweater and bra had disappeared. Charles licked at her nipples like a pup you might see in a pet store window. This tickled, and excited her as well. She made sounds—he worried that he might be hurting her but she reassured him—and then she was thinking, Oh, my God, I'm here with this guy and it's only because we're the same height.

"No, please, no," she said, taking him by the wrist and settling his hands back in his lap. Sitting there, naked to the waist, she felt a little chill—goosebumps!—but no embarrassment or shame.

"Jas," he said.

"I can't," she said.

"What's wrong?" He tried to look her in the eye but his glance kept slipping.

"Nothing's wrong. It's just not right."

He wasn't happy about this, but he stood up—a gentleman, which almost won Jas over, but she managed to stand, or sit, her ground. He adjusted his clothing while she scrambled into her sweater. After a few more words he allowed her to usher him out of the apartment. After she shut the door she pressed her ear to the wood and listened to his footsteps fade away down the stairs. She paced around the living room awhile, wondering if she had done the wrong thing. At the window she watched the spinning leaves, a car passing by, another car. A hooded man on a bicycle. Two late-night strollers. No one, for minutes. The bicyclist circled back. A car rolled past from the opposite direction.

Finally, she dragged herself to bed, lying there in the dark while the night sounds magnified. When she jumped at what sounded like the crack of a stick in the street—who knew what that cracking noise meant?—the clock at her bedside showed only the next half hour. At the noise of her intercom, she jumped to her feet and went to the door. The buzzing came again, steady and insistent. Going to the window, she saw no movement on the street except the blowing leaves. The buzzer again. Back at the door, she took a deep breath and pushed the button.

She listened carefully as the street door opened and then thudded closed. Footsteps on the stairs. It seemed like several minutes before the climber reached her landing.

"Jas?" from the other side of the door.

"Who is it?"

Squinting through the peephole, she could scarcely make him out. "Charles?"

Slowly she opened the door to face him, leaving it on the chain.

"Oh, my God," she said, seeing his bleeding forehead and his bloodied hand cupped over his nose.

He'd been sitting on the stoop, he said. Hadn't gone home when she'd kicked him out.

"But why?"

"How am I supposed to know?" He shook his head before the mirror, studying his sorry face.

Jas handed him a hot damp towel.

A hooded man on a bicycle had swung past the stoop, made a quick turn, and let the bike fall onto the sidewalk as he charged, slamming Charles in the face and grabbing his wallet.

"We need to call the police," Jas said, watching him dab the deep red smears across his cheeks.

"No, no," Charles shook his head. His voice wasn't his own, it was so nasal because of his smashed, bleeding nose. "More trouble than it's worth. I'll cancel my credit cards. I didn't have that much cash." He stopped and studied his contorted face in the mirror. "No driver's license."

"You don't drive?"

"Never learned," he said, resuming his work with the towel. "Easy here. I take cabs. I take the Metro. Soon as I clean up I'll call myself a cab. Should have done that in the first place, I guess."

"No," Jas said. "It's so late." With a sigh she pulled her robe close and left the bathroom for the hall, opening the closet and dragging out some bedding that she carried into the front room and tossed onto the sofa.

"Thanks," he said, having followed her from the bathroom. "I really appreciate this." He was staring at the bedding as if sheer will alone might help to arrange it as Jas left the room. While she lay there in the dark in her own bed she heard him adjust and readjust himself on the sofa. The apartment walls creaked, but the sound didn't seem so menacing now that she was not alone.

He coughed.

She breathed deeply, trying to ignore his presence. A car passed by on the street below. The wind rattled the trees. Her breathing softened.

But at the feel of weight on the bed she sat up alert, awake.

Charles leaned over her, his breath sour and metallic from the beer and the blood.

"I have a confession to make," he said.

In the light from the other room his head seemed to quiver slightly as he spoke, as though he suffered from the onset of some neurological condition.

"Are you all right?" Jas asked.

"I have to tell you this," Charles said, leaning toward her.

"What?"

"I lied," he said.

"What?"

"I wasn't mugged."

"What are you saying?"

"I wasn't mugged. I punched myself in the nose with my own fist. That's how bad I was feeling."

"Get out, please," Jas said. "I need to sleep."

"I'm sorry," he said. "There was a black guy on a bike and he looked pretty menacing. He kept circling the block. I was afraid to walk home. It'll be worse now."

"Get out!" she said in a voice so strident that a few hours later when she awoke and dressed for work her throat still felt raw. Charles, of course, was gone, having left sometime between that terrible moment and the onset of the muted late winter dawn.

With a cup of strong coffee in hand she stalked around the apartment, sniffing, sniffing, as if she might find out the part of herself that seemed to have melted away in the throes of the night. With the cup half empty she sat down and toyed with the telephone, dialing part of her father's number and then breaking off the call. She tried Sharon.

Please leave a message when you hear the beep for either . . .

She broke that connection, too. Who wanted to hear Sharon's name entwined electronically or otherwise with that bald-headed eagle Fletcher? It made Jas wonder. It made her shiver. It made her jealous. But she wasn't giving in to anything. Jumping to her feet, she swept up her coat from the closet, propelled herself out the door, and climbed down the stairs. Halfway down she stopped, cursed herself, and climbed back up to fetch her forgotten briefcase. Then she headed down again, her heart racing.

Her walk to the office, which she had lately come to enjoy despite the lingering cold weather, was this morning a torture. Low clouds pressed down, seeming to touch the tops of the marble buildings, wind slashing across Pennsylvania Avenue, attacking her face and ears. A voice in her ear: her father's. Saying what? She couldn't quite make it out over the noise of the wind and the passing cars. At the corner, by a line of newspaper vending machines, Jas stopped, waiting for the traffic light to change.

PRESIDENT SMILES ON—

—she caught a glimpse of a headline. On? On what? She would have searched for a coin for the vending machine but the light changed in her favor and she crossed the street. A few guards stood about laughing and joking, white breath to the wind, at the rear of the Library of Congress. Jas pushed ahead, eyes on the sidewalk the rest of the block.

At the office Charles was not around.

When Jas inquired about him in what she hoped was her most offhand manner, Carla the receptionist said he might be at the Budget Office.

There was snow coming, she told Jas. A late storm. And did she see the paper about another mugging on the hill—a black man on a bicycle had clobbered some young secretary on her way home and taken her money and keys.

"The money part I don't care about," Carla said. "But the keys? What do you do without your keys?"

Jas stood quietly, listening.

"Oh, and *he* wants to see you," Carla added, holding up a memo. "Just buzzed me. Got some bug up his gazoobee this morning." She narrowed her eyes in a way Jas had never noticed before and said, "Watch yourself."

"Watch myself? Is there something wrong?"

Carla shook her head mysteriously, suggesting with a nod that Jas had better get moving.

"Just watch yourself," she said.

A telephone rang. Two telephones rang behind her.

"I'm going," Jas said, heading for the door leading to her boss's domain. A door slammed ahead of her and she met the brawny national correspondent, whose eyes registered a faint sign of recognition.

"He's all yours," he said, passing her on the run, the faint odor of his breath lingering in the air. Jas turned to watch him go and caught him looking back at her.

"Do you do research?" he said.

Before Jas could reply he said, "I need someone. If you're interested, give me a call."

Jas shook off the suggestion and went directly to the Senator's door.

"Come in," he called when he saw her standing there. "And close it."

She stepped inside and drew the door closed behind her, feeling the pull of his eyes. A lingering trace of the correspondent's breath yielded to the powerful odor of the Senator's cologne.

"I like to check with new staff—with everybody who works here— every once in a while." The Senator bore in on her with those eyes, and Jas made it a point of pride that she didn't turn away.

"I've been watching you," he said, "ever since that day in the tunnel."

"We met before that once, sir," Jas said. "At a party—"

"I go to too many parties," the Senator said as he stood and walked around to the front of his desk. Jas was half a head taller than the man and when he approached her she could look down through the rectangular pattern of his thinning hair and see the shining—lacquered almost—surface of his scalp. In that instant the Senator seemed to lean toward her and almost as if in some practiced move from an athletic competition suddenly thrust his arms around her, at the same time raising his mouth toward hers. Before she could register what was happening his tongue slipped in between her teeth.

"Uh," Jas made a sound as she pulled her mouth from his. But she couldn't get further back—he had her trapped, bumping his belly against her pelvis.

"Please," she said, finally tearing herself free.

"Wait," the Senator said as she went for the door. He grabbed her by the shoulders, pulling her back toward him, nuzzling his mouth against the back of her neck. Jas wrenched herself loose, yanking open the door as he whispered an apology behind her, and flung herself into the hall.

She spent the rest of the day at the Library of Congress—beneath it, to be exact—wandering the tunnels from building to building, stopping in a snack room for a soda and a bag of chips, then setting out again, getting as far as the next set of elevators before turning and walking back through the long wide passageway, listening to the echoes of voices and the nattering of machines. Up and along the wide corridors she dawdled, strolled, slowed to notice marked and unmarked doors along the walls, then hurried along again, changing direction, following arrows, marking her pathway by the signs on the walls. The traffic around her ebbed and flowed.

When from a long distance she saw a tall man in a great hurry coming toward her, she turned and picked up her pace. A pair of hooded workers pushed a long cart ahead of her and she ducked around them to step into a narrow passageway to the left where sawhorses and old steel bookshelves stood haphazardly along the wall. Someone called to her and she hurried along. Spying one of those doors in the wall, she stopped to pull it open. It opened—luck or stupidity or ineptitude or policy had left it unlocked—and she stepped inside, closing the door behind her. Pipes and machinery murmured overhead, all around her. Standing in the dark, hugging her arms to her chest, she heard voices raised in laughter in the narrow hall outside. She began to shudder in a sort of cold and voiceless misery, her tall body bending forward and jerking back as though she were controlled by some puppetmaster much taller than she who yanked her on a string.

In her ear a noise, a whisper, a voice: her father's. Home, it was saying, how he needed her, the safety would be a luxury but one she deserved. It became garbled then, muffled and distorted by her own sobs and coughs. One last word she could make out: swan. And she was overtaken by a series of wracking cries so deep they seemed to come up from her ankles and knees rather than her belly and chest.

The light flooded over her.

A dark man in green sweatshirt and voluminous black trousers stood in the doorway not three feet away.

"What you doing here?"

Her heart jammed in her chest; her breathing eased only when she saw the chain around his neck with the dangling ID card that caught the reflection of the bright bulbs overhead.

"I don't know," she said. "I don't know."

Tallgrass Prairie

Light browns and dark, leaves and turned earth, on the far horizon a water tower with the name of the town becoming clear as the car rumbled closer.

"I've been here before," Goldstad said, turning slightly in his seat to address the plain-faced woman behind the wheel.

"When was that?" she said. "Really?"

"Not here. In the other one."

"Oh, in the Mediterranean! Jim and I always talk about going there some time. Imagine, living most of your adult life in a town with the same name but never going to its namesake. But he does his work up in Alaska . . . Or did . . ."

"Our glacier man," Goldstad said.

"Do you know his work? He's certainly an admirer of yours." The woman glanced at him, then back to the road.

"I look forward to meeting him," Goldstad said, associating the lie with the immediate onset of one of those headaches he'd been pounded by for months.

"He wanted to meet your plane but he had a medical appointment in town that he couldn't break. You'll meet him at the reception."

"That's before the lecture?"

"Yes," the woman said, steering the car past a road sign that announced the city limits. "And another one after."

"You do it up big here in Crete," he said.

"We try," the woman said, giving him what appeared to be her best smile.

Her husband, the glacier man, arrived at the small reception a bit late looking rather red-faced in jacket and tie—the only other person in the room in such attire besides Goldstad himself. He apologized for his tardiness and asked Goldstad about some biographical details he wanted to get right for his introduction.

"You wrote *Atlantis on Our Minds* when you were only twenty-five, correct?"

Goldstad nodded, sipping near-sour red wine from a plastic glass. He had cadged an aspirin from the glacier man's wife when they had first come in to the reception, but it didn't seem to help. The battering about his temples had increased as soon as he had walked into the room where tired teachers in rumpled clothes stood about quietly chatting, without much to distinguish them from the students he had noticed on the path from the parking lot to the low red-brick building except perhaps less hair and more wrinkles.

"And then came—?" The glacier man named two more titles, not in the right order. Goldstad corrected him and swallowed his wine. He was looking around for the bar when a rough-skinned fellow wearing a leather vest, his dark hair twisted into a single braid that lay on his left shoulder like a dead snake, offered to fetch him another.

"Guy Perkins," the man said, offering his hand when he returned with another plastic glass of wine. "Land management theory."

Goldstad accepted both the hand and the wine.

"You know, I'm a really big fan of *Sixty Million Buffalo*," said the man with the braid.

"Thank you," Goldstad said, tasting the sour drink on his tongue.

He met several more members of the science faculty and a tall woman with almond-shaped eyes and a bust that sloped attractively beneath her white jersey, "a poet with an interest in science" was the way she introduced herself.

"Can I get you anything?" she said.

Suddenly it was dark, the pale sun having slipped westward into the Platte River basin, and he was sitting in a booth in a dimly lighted bar across from the man with the braid and the tall poet with the liquid motion to her breasts. Billiard balls clicked against each other near the rear of the long room.

"I'm looking forward to your lecture," the poet spoke up.

"Me, too," Goldstad said, feeling the touch of a foot beneath the table.

"But seriously," the braid man said, "it's a great title, 'Tallgrass Prairie and the—'"

"I don't mean to cut you off," Goldstad said, "but do either of you happen to have an aspirin?"

"I might," the poet said, reaching for her bag and peering inside. "Here." She handed him a small jar of tablets.

Goldstad took several of the pills from the bottle and washed them down with his sweet barroom wine.

"Now," he said. "I hope I haven't insulted the glacier man by having slipped away with you two."

"The glacier man?" the poet said.

"Jim, he means Jim," the braid man said. "He'll be fine. He's probably in the men's room right now rehearsing his introduction."

"His wife picked me up at the airport. He had a medical appointment."

"Three times a week," the braid man said. "He's on dialysis."

IN THE CAR on the way back to the campus—a two-minute ride—he listened to his stomach growl over the noise of the engine.

"I've forgotten to eat dinner," he said.

The tall poet leaned an arm over the back of her seat and said, "Finger food at the party after the lecture. All you can eat."

But first he had to give the talk.

"Not since Buckminster Fuller . . ." the glacier man said from the lectern, giving the appearance of being in every way normal—still in his coat and tie, slightly graying at the temples, thick plastic temple pieces holding his eyeglasses that caught the reflection of the spotlights.

Goldstad leaned forward and touched his forehead to the cool brick of the backstage wall. From his pocket he extracted the bottle of pills the poet had given him, opened it quickly, and shook two loose into his palm. Applause echoed through the hall and Goldstad pushed himself away from the wall and stepped out into the light, furiously chewing. He mumbled a thank you to the glacier man as they passed in midstage and took charge of the lectern, staring into the glare as he found a glass of water and washed down the gritty residue in his throat.

In an hour he was done, with little recollection of what he had said except that it all sounded to him quite familiar. The applause went on for several minutes. Someone near the rear of the hall whistled sharply, as if calling a dog. Led by the glacier man, Goldstad left the stage and walked up the long aisle to the rear of the hall and out into the lobby where he took a place at a table and began signing books.

"And you are—?" he said to the tall woman leaning over him, her breasts shifting beneath the pure white jersey.

"Very funny," she said.

"But your name?"

She told him and he immediately forgot, inscribing her copy of *Atlantis on Our Minds*—a hardcover copy, not a paperback—in a vague flattering way. She stepped back from the table, allowing the next person in line—a bearded young student with a wide grin on his face—to hold up his book.

"See you at the party," she said.

He noticed her there on the other side of the room in the small frame prairie gothic structure that belonged to the Dean and his wife, a smiling pair, he in a thick wool suit and gold-rimmed glasses similar to Goldstad's and she in a blue dress with a white collar so far out of style that it had come back in style again. Sliced meat and cheese were spread on white plates atop a table covered with a red cloth. Goldstad ate little. Though the wine tasted sour, he kept on drinking. After several glasses, he cleared his throat and the hovering guests fell silent. He made an impromptu speech about the danger of the right wing to North American ecology and the danger of the left wing to South American ecology. The Dean edged away from him as he spoke while the braid man delivered another drink. Goldstad looked around for the tall poet, thinking he caught a glimpse of her passing by the door to the kitchen.

The glacier man drove him back along the now-dark county road to his hotel in the nearby state capital.

"Your introduction was quite generous," Goldstad said.

"I'm a great admirer of yours," the man said.

Goldstad watched the trees go by, shadows in the dark clumped above the vacant fields.

"To tell you the truth," he said, "I've put that particular work behind me."

"I imagined you'd be writing something new, of course," the driver said.

"Yes, I am."

"And?"

"Oh, you want to know. Now that you're pressing me on it—"

"I honestly don't mean to press you."

"By all means, press," Goldstad said. "If I could tell you, I would. But I've only just begun to think about it."

"And can you tell me a little about it?"

"I wish I knew," Goldstad said. "A memoir, perhaps."

"A memoir?"

"I don't know what else to call it. It's just sort of hit me that that's what I should do."

"And I was present when the idea came to you?"

"You're my witness."

The driver made no sound but Goldstad could feel a certain effulgence flowing out from his body in the dark, as though the man's pleasure had suddenly taken shape and form.

"May I ask you something?"

"Of course," the glacier man said.

Goldstad glanced back into the dark and threw out the question.

"What is it like?"

"What is what like?"

Goldstad took a breath.

"Your treatment."

"My treatment?"

"Dialysis," Goldstad said, keeping his eye on the road. On the far horizon a red light winked on and off, on and off, obviously a warning to low-flying airplanes.

"Going there, you mean?"

"No, not the mechanics of it," Goldstad said. "The feeling of it."

"Well . . . why, you feel . . . this is going to sound too simple but it's true . . . you feel . . . connected. A certain slipping away of all ties but at the same time you have a powerful awareness of being . . ." He paused and took a breath. "Do you have children?"

"No," Goldstad said. "Never had."

"We have a couple of teenagers," the man said. "And they say, when they do what we used to call 'falling for somebody' or 'getting involved' with somebody, they say 'hooked up.' 'I'm hooked up with Margie, Dad,' my boy'll say. And that's how it feels to me on that machine. I'm hooked up and I'm literally and figuratively 'hooked up,' if you know what I mean."

"I think so," Goldstad said.

"And when that blood river returns to me," the driver said, his voice taking on a new and somewhat troubling urgency now that he seemed to understand what Goldstad had asked for, "when the blood returns to my veins, I feel almost as though I'm drowning. It's a feeling of sinking down down down into a surging tide and feeling myself carried along, with fierce winds at my back, and, I swear, my entire life comes back to me . . ."

"The first time?"

"Every time," the man said. "Do you know how high the suicide rate is for people on the machine? The psychologists say it's because of a feeling of uselessness, but I don't think so, not for me, it's not. So my field work days are over. I've got data enough for the rest of my life. As long as it lasts. My life, that is. But there's always that urge to make an end to it all and I think it comes from the fact that you're so used to dying every time you're hooked up to the machine you know it's not all that hard to cross over the line."

Streetlamps flickered on either side of the road; the city streets reverberated beneath their wheels. He noticed storefronts, a restaurant, a clothing store, a bank, a business supply store—all closed—and as they turned the corner a neon sign of dancing girls winked on and off with the same frequency as the red light atop the decorative tower of the state capitol—the glacier man announced the landmark to him as they approached it. Within moments they pulled up alongside the entrance to the hotel, all new brick in the style of a frontier facade.

Now the glacier man had questions for him, and Goldstad sat in the car with the engine running, talking about his old project, the campaign to reseed the old tallgrass prairie across the southern plains. Why, yes, a man had to sit high in the saddle of a tall horse just to see over the top of the grass! Sixty million buffalo rumbled through his disquisition and as he talked he could almost smell deep in his nostrils the smoke of a thousand natural burns. All the way through the lobby and up in the elevator that lifted him to the highest floor of the hotel, the odor stayed with him.

Shutting the door of his room behind him, he sat on his bed in his coat and tie and shoes, breathing hard. Outside the window the blinking light atop the capitol intermittently announced its presence for anyone who cared to observe. The dancing girls sign burned on and off in his mind. Almost as if on signal his headache—familiar antagonist by now—returned with a stunning blow to his right temple. He fetched a glass of water from the bathroom sink and washed down the remaining tablet from the now empty bottle. He hovered in the center of the room like an intruder in his own space, his shoulders heaving up and down with the soundless progress of his breath.

The telephone rang once, then stopped. He walked to the desk and picked up the receiver, heard the droning of a dial tone, set it down again. Sitting at the desk, he reached into his briefcase, took out his notebook, and began to write.

Kitty and I had been married for about six years at the time of our trip to Crete. Our marriage might have appeared solid to look at it from the outside. Many marriages do. Bitter clashes broke out between us at the slightest provocation. Her painting, which had attracted me to her while she was still a student, had slowed to a halt. Our trip came about because I had suggested that some time spent in the Mediterranean might reinvigorate her eye. She considered this, argued with me, finally accepted the idea of it. All across Italy we argued bitterly about nothing. On the island the sea and the stones and the sun seemed to distract us for a while. We spent mornings at our separate labors, she with her pastels and me with my notebook. In the afternoons—

A knock at the door interrupted him.
"Yes?"
He got up to answer it.

"Room service," said the uniformed young man, handing him a small yellow tin of aspirin.

"I didn't order this," Goldstad said. "But I need it. Thanks."

He took the tin and stared a moment at the fellow's outstretched hand before finding a bill in his wallet and handing it over. After shutting the door he returned to the bathroom where he poured himself another glass of water and washed down two of the pills before going back to the desk and picking up the pen.

> *. . . when she thought I was asleep she sat up quietly and slipped out of bed. I opened one eye and saw her standing at the window as if to signal someone on the street below or perhaps looking for a signal. In a moment she turned to pull a sweater from the chair where she had tossed it and left the room, closing the door with a stealth I hadn't known she was capable of. I waited for a half minute or so and then climbed out of bed and followed her out the door. She had reached the stairs before I got to the end of the hall. A teenage boy was working the night shift behind the small desk. When he saw me, he immediately pointed to the front door as though he had been expecting my arrival soon after her departure.*

Writing the last sentence sent something like an electric current running through his arm and up along his shoulder. He stood up, as if to relieve a cramp. His head throbbed, especially at the right temple. Pressing his palm against the outward wall of pain, he stood there a moment listening to himself breathe, and then sat down again.

He wrote:

> *I hurried onto the dirt road and saw—*

"Kitty!"

The sound of his own voice shocked him and he sighed and leaned hard against the back of the chair, staring out the window for what seemed to be several minutes before he returned to the notebook.

—and followed her onto the jetty that jutted out into the crashing surf. There was a bright moon whose light split into particles, breaking over rocks, the tops of waves, on the silver ring I bought her in Athens in the hope that it might show her what I still felt about her, this ring that caught the moonlight as she waved to the lone figure who stood waiting at the end of the pier of rocks. I stopped and crouched down in the moonlight, not that they, caught up as they were in their passion, would have seen me. The young man dressed all in white who by some trick of the night glow appeared at this distance to be all dark in my eyes, my wife Kitty—Kitty!—rushing to embrace him. They sank down onto the rocks and proceeded to undress, flinging clothes in all directions. Careful, I said to them in my mind, the wind will carry something off into the sea . . .

The telephone rang and he reached for it.
"Hello?"
"Hi."
"Who is this?"
"How soon we forget."
"Who—?"
"'A woman of mystery.'"
"Did you call a while ago?"
"No."
"Did you tell room service to send me up some aspirin?"
He could hear her breathing at the other end of the line. She said, "Yes."
"I should thank you."
"Then thank me," she said.

"All right then. Thank you."

"And?"

"Where are you?" he said.

"Where do you think?"

"In the lobby?"

"Brilliant deduction."

"Would you like to come up?" he said without much hesitation.

"If you tell me your room number, I might consider it."

Goldstad, who was usually plagued by the recollection of useless numbers, had to consult his room card.

"I live just a few blocks away," she said when she appeared at the door. "This is on my way home."

"You could have driven me," he said.

"Jim wanted to. He would have been disappointed."

"That's right," Goldstad said.

"You're writing," she said, going up to the desk.

"Just some notes," he said.

"Did the aspirin help?" Her voice, which had risen a touch a moment ago, now sank back to its normal level.

"Seems to have," he said.

"I brought something else," she said.

"What's that?'

"You're a big endorser of weeds. I brought some with me."

"I'm finished with weeds," he said.

"You spoke of them quite eloquently this evening," she said.

"That's show business," he said.

"Well, do you mind if I indulge a bit?"

"You're my guest. So be my guest."

She shrugged, sat down on the edge of his bed and dug into her bag. In a few minutes smoke encircled them like a wide filmy net. She offered, he accepted, puffed, coughed, inhaled, coughed, then lay back on the bed at an odd angle alongside her.

"What are you writing?" she said in a voice quite different from either the high or the low tone she had used before.

"My memoirs," he said.

"Will they come this far?" she said.

"Not as far as you."

BY THE EARLY light she was gone and he was left with such a headache that within the space of another hour he had finished off half the tin of aspirin. His stomach churned and he sat, futilely, on the commode, waiting for something to happen. Eventually he showered and dressed. At the window he noticed clouds, faint sun rising, cars rolling toward a traffic light just below his room. A bank rooftop parking lot was empty except for a lone white van coated with a faint sheen of frost. He touched his face and realized that he had forgotten to shave. No time seemed to pass—he was standing before the window watching the increase of the light—when the call came from the lobby.

"I'm here," said the voice he recognized as belonging to the glacier man's wife.

A veil of snow fluttered against the window while he finished packing.

"I want to apologize again for Jim's absence," she said when he met her in the lobby.

"I understand," he said, following her to the car she had left at the curb and tossing his bag into the back of the vehicle.

Snow fell lightly on the windshield as he climbed into the passenger seat. Trees stood ghostly behind a flimsy blowing curtain of snow as they drove out of town.

"Tell him again how much I appreciated his introduction," he said, watching the weather spin up around them .

"It was an honor for him," she said. "For us."

"Thank you, and I was pleased to be invited."

The woman removed a hand from the steering wheel and reached into the large satchel that rested on the seat between them. "We wanted you to have something," she said.

"Really?"

"I never told you what I do."

"I never asked," he said. "And I'm sorry."

"No, no, that's not why I'm telling you this. I'm a collector. And I sell."

"And what do you collect and sell?"

"Oh," she said. "Things. Collectors' items, sort of. Prairie oddments."

"Prairie oddments?"

"Well," she said, "we wanted you to have this." She handed over a small white object.

"It's real horn," she said as he weighed the beautifully carved buffalo in his palm.

"I . . . can't accept this," he said.

"Please do," she said.

He closed his hand around it, then stowed it in his jacket pocket.

Signs for the airport loomed ahead. He watched for the entryway for his airline.

"Here we are," she said.

"Well, thank you," he said. "Thank you very much."

He offered his hand in farewell.

"I'll wait with you," she said.

"Oh, I'll be fine," he said, staring off into the thickening bluster of snow.

"What if they cancel your flight?"

"I'll call if that happens," he said. "But I don't think that's going to happen, do you?"

"The weather is strange," she said.

"But not worse than Alaska."

"Oh, no," she said. "Not worse than that."

"I better go then," he said, inclining his head toward her as if to say thanks one more time. The snow swirled about him as he stood at the rear of the vehicle waiting for her to undo the latch so that he might pick up his bag. He raised a hand to wave as she drove away from the curb and then hitched the bag to his shoulder.

Inside the terminal he checked in at his airline counter and then found a drinking fountain and swallowed several aspirin. He sat in one of the uncomfortable plastic chairs at his gate and wrote in his notebook for the next half hour and when they announced his flight he kept the book under his arm so that he could get to work immediately after takeoff. He watched with interest from his window seat as a man in dark clothes sitting in a large vehicle worked the long arms of a machine resembling a tall mower or reaper that cleansed the wing of ice. The flight attendants gave instructions. Buckled into his seat, he fumbled in his jacket pocket for a pen. His fingers found the little object the glacier man's wife had given him and he rubbed it and caressed it. The plane began to roll along the runway as snow angled against it like confetti tossed by a bunch of very large children running alongside. Lifting, the airplane tilted against the sporadic bursts of white. Suddenly they slipped into the clouds and the whine of the engines subsided into a smooth rumble. As if they were rising through many fathoms of water the airplane drifted up to meet and pass through the yellow-gold undercoating of the clouds until sunlight spread across the sky.

Someone in the seat behind him rustled a newspaper. A passenger coughed, a signal for another to make a loud, vaudeville-like yawn. A tone sounded through the cabin. A flight attendant hurried along the aisle in a whisper of trouser-legs trailed by the light but insistent odor of soap. Reaching into his pocket, Goldstad retrieved the small white buffalo and admired it in the light of the brilliant sun, running his finger across its incised surface and along its curves. He leaned toward the window, trying to catch a glimpse of the passing earth.

Apache Woods

Danny Crowther (born Danny Kravitz) had flown into Albuquerque for a few days in order to sort things out. But he was still feeling like a migrant as he rolled south on Interstate 25 in a wind-shaken van driven by his former girl friend Helen. Her black-bearded husband Barry hunched forward in the seat behind him—so that you can get the full effect of the view, Bar had said when he offered Danny the front passenger seat—and asked him, "What exactly do you do?"

Though he knew his silence might be taken as rude, Danny didn't answer right away. The sky spread out all around them, dark thunderheads stitching up from the horizon to the east while ahead of them to the south remained a dome of perfect pale blue, almost turquoise. He was lost in it for a time, this space, this color. The turquoise reminded him of the eyes of an actress he had dated for several months last year. She had left him for a man who owned livery companies. Danny had become a lot richer than that guy, at least up until this week when questions had arisen in certain quarters about some of his holdings, but the girl still hadn't returned his calls.

He glanced over at Helen, her odd irregular face, lines scored in it by the sun, her raven hair roughed about by the wind. She worked the pedals with her feet in running shoes; a few inches of textured black stocking showed below the cuffs of her jeans.

"I buy and sell," Danny said, finally, as much to Helen as to her husband.

Bar leaned close to his ear.

"You wouldn't want to buy a Little Professor Bookstore franchise in Albuquerque, would you?"

"Are you asking or telling?" Danny said. "Who knows? I love books. I was an English major. Ask Helen. I read poetry. Wallace Stevens is one of my favorites. What's that line? Something, something, something, on extended wings . . . ?"

He twisted around and looked his bearded host in the eye.

"So how's your store doing? Had it long?"

"A few years now," Bar said.

"What's your inventory worth?"

"Gentlemen," said Helen from behind the wheel, "this is a pleasure trip. Danny, when you turned up at the airport last night you said you came for a little rest. So stop dealing and rest."

"Right," Danny said, looking to the side of the road. "*Socorro*," he read on a sign.

He cleared his throat, feeling again the burning sensation that had plagued him all week. "Why do I know that name?"

"It means 'help,'" Helen said.

"So let's stop here," Danny said. "I need all the help I can get." He heard Bar make a sound as if to speak and took a breath himself—he did need help with this terrible sore throat that burned each time he swallowed. "Actually, I have to piss."

A gas station appeared within the next mile. Helen steered the van up to the low white building. Danny got out, and Bar followed him into the dark washroom that gave off an odor as awful as anything Danny had ever smelled. Standing there before the clay-colored urinal, he suffered a pain so sharp that at first he thought Bar might have stabbed him in the back. When he got to L.A., he decided, he was going to have to turn himself over to a doctor who would have shots for this thing that burned when he swallowed and burned when he pissed—whatever this thing was. Walking back to the van with Bar he scarcely heard the man talk about the sights that lay in store for them in the sanctuary down the road, reviewing in his mind the girls who might be responsible, if it was a girl. If it was something else he didn't know what to think.

For the next few miles, Danny began to notice white spots on the horizon, flashes, probably, from passing airplanes and automobiles. Lonely hills, the beginnings of mountains, loomed beyond the tablelands. He could see those clearly against the fine turquoise sky, so it wasn't his eyes, those flecks of brilliance. In the dry heat of the vehicle sweat trickled down the sides of his chest. In Chicago, on the way to catch his connection to the coast, he had seen the placard for the flight to Albuquerque and walked up to the counter and changed his ticket. A great surge of heat in his chest at the time made him think that Albuquerque would be a good place to stop and stay still. Now that they sat in silence he wondered if his judgment might be skewed. Yet there was Helen's face. He swallowed more fire, feeling the pressure of the last few weeks like the kind of corset men wear when they have injured their backs. After a while Helen took her foot off the gas pedal, allowing the van to stammer and slow in the wind.

"The turnoff," she said, pointing to a sign that Danny, usually alert to such things, had swung around too late to read. He didn't miss the figures chalked on the sign at the entrance to the sanctuary: Snow geese, 35,000. There were other birds listed, but the snow geese stood out because of their numbers.

"*Bosque del Apache*," Bar said from behind him. "Apache Woods to you."

"You never used to watch birds back in Jersey," Danny said as Helen navigated the dirt road along the edge of a marsh surprisingly large given the aridity of the region they had passed through.

"In Jersey, as I remember it," Helen said, "all the birds were dead." She reached down and switched off the ignition.

"It's a new life out here for her," Bar said. There was a lightness to his voice that seemed odd considering the great bulk of his body. Danny let his mind work just for an instant on what Bar and Helen might be like together, but immediately pulled back. The stink of the marsh, bitter, moist, upset his fantasy. Here and there delicate white-feathered fowl thin as sticks stalked among the reeds in the muck near the shore. Cries and honks, shrieks and yips filled the air. A tremulous white carpet covered the far section of the pond.

"Bar," Helen said after they had walked about a quarter of a mile up the red mud of the track, "I've forgotten the binocs *and* the sandwiches. Could you?"

Her large husband nodded sweetly and turned back toward the van.

Danny cleared his throat and spit. Perhaps a dozen hawks lazed overhead in circles one atop the other. He kicked at the mud. Sweat trickled down his back and his tongue felt like dirt.

Helen touched him on the arm.

"So you're not married?"

Danny shook his head.

"I was, but I'm not now."

"Well, I am now," Helen said.

"I noticed," Danny said.

"Notice this?"

Without any warning, Helen pulled loose the front hem of her blouse and quickly unzipped and and yanked down the front of her jeans, showing him the half-moon crescent of the scar just below the waistline of her dark tights. She must have heard the noise he made in his throat, because she said, "You didn't think it would go away, did you?"

Danny was about to say something, though he wasn't sure what, but at that moment Bar called out to them from down the trail where he was pointing toward the marsh. A large, red-tufted crane, as beautiful and mysterious as anything Danny had ever seen, stood poised at the edge of the reeds.

Bearded Bar stalked toward them and handed over two pairs of binoculars. Helen took hers and wandered up the path, her clothing somehow miraculously back in place. The two men stared at the bird and then at each other. There came a clap or a shout, a backfire from a car or truck—game warden, Bar said hastily—at the north edge of the marsh, and then a rumbling unrolled across the water. Bar motioned to Danny who clamped the binoculars to his eyes, then let them drop to his side. The sound! Forty or fifty thousand wings lifting off almost all at once. The sound seemed to roar out of the trembling light, the sky itself finally coming undone and soaring off toward the west.

ON THE RETURN trip north Danny finally coughed up a little information. "I'm having some trouble with numbers," he said.

"What does that mean?" Helen spoke without looking over at him. Daylight was fading fast. To their right, the east, lights blinked on along the hills back from the highway. It all seemed to work with the synchronicity of a stage set, the broad sky dimming, the tiny lights winking on—and Danny, once a great fan of the theater, found that he was hamming it up a little, for Helen's sake.

"Oh, there's some guys want to talk to me, something about a problem with inside trading." His hands fluttered around him as he spoke, like living creatures set loose within the van. "They come to you, they talk, they go away, then they say they're coming back, then they—"

"You're one of *those* guys," Bar said. "You must be nervous. I'd be nervous. So—hey?—are you, like, here to hide out?"

It was a bum question, a stupid question to come from a man who appeared to have some sense. But Danny kept his temper. He spoke calmly, recalling that moment at O'Hare.

"I was on my way to catch the plane to L.A., and I saw the flight to Albuquerque, and I said to myself, Hey, I'm a big boy, I can do anything I want, so if I want to stop off and see my old friend Helen, that's allowed, isn't it? So that's when I called."

Helen drove on silently, as if she were not a main figure in his story, staring at the dark roadway now only barely illuminated by the beams from the van. The faint blue light on the western horizon seemed to pulse brighter but quickly faded. Each time Danny looked it had turned an increment darker. *Socorro.* They passed that marker again, and when Danny looked this time the west had grown as dark as the east, darker, since there were no sparkling patches of lights, signals of farms and towns.

A good dinner—Helen had learned to cook Southwest style, and Danny found this to his liking, the subtle, often biting hot spices, the graininess of the tortillas, the smoothness of the cheese and avocado. They washed it all down with tangy cold beer. He ate a great deal and drank too many beers, and at what was an early hour for him he excused himself and made for the little guest house on the patio where they had put him the night before. He stumbled at the doorstep, waving his hand through the ceramic chimes in the shapes of fish that dangled alongside the entrance to the little house.

"You need some help?"

Helen's voice floated across the patio. But when he turned, she was ducking in the doorway of the main house. He stood there, swaying in the dark, and then went inside and fell across the bed.

He awoke in his clothes to sunlight, birdsong, a breeze in the chimes. He needed a telephone. He had spent an entire day without using a telephone. Smoothing out his clothes, he stepped out onto the patio to find Helen in a black bikini sitting on a lawn chair in the middle of a stone garden. His throat burned when he cleared it, as though the light itself had penetrated the soft tissue beneath his chin. Helen wore dark glasses. Danny couldn't tell whether or not she followed his gaze to the scar, looking now like a child's attempt at a figure eight, showing above the rim of cloth that masked her groin from the sun. She held a book open on her chest, the front, spine, back cover facing out at Danny, the author's dour, creased face, the vertical title on the spine repeated again horizontally on the front cover: *Twilight* by Elie Wiesel.

"What's that about?" Danny moved closer.

"The destruction of the Jews," Helen said.

He blinked at the sun, stared down at her again.

"I've got enough trouble being me."

Helen put a finger in her place and closed the book on her lap.

"What exactly is it, Dan?"

He turned at the sound of the wind chimes.

"The details wouldn't mean anything to you," he said. "It would be like a doctor telling me about my insides when all I needed to know about was the cure."

"There's a cure for you?"

Helen smiled her old, mysterious smile.

"I've got a lawyer working on a cure—"

"Not a doctor?"

Helen set the book on the stones next to her chair and crossed her glistening legs.

"Would you like some breakfast? Bar made some coffee before he left."

"A thoughtful guy," Danny said. "Where'd he go? The store open this early on a Sunday?"

Helen shook her head. "It's not that early. But he doesn't go to the store until later. Until after his meeting."

Danny took a breath. He hadn't realized until then how tense and poised he stood.

"What is he, a Quaker?"

Helen laughed, a sound that Danny had often listened to before this.

"He's at the congregation," she said. "He's on the executive committee."

"I didn't even think he was Jewish," Danny said.

"He wasn't when we met. He is now."

"You're playing games. You mean, he converted?"

"Is that so amazing?"

Danny found his eyes wandering to the scar again.

"So what does that mean? That he had to take classes?"

Helen nodded.

"And what else?" Danny said. "Did he have to get himself . . . clipped?"

She laughed again, and he found himself annoyed that he was interested in the noise she made in her throat.

"Danny," she said, "most American men are already . . . clipped."

"Oh, you been making a survey?"

She blinked at him.

"Would you like some coffee?"

"I'll get some coffee," he said, turning to walk back across the patio into the house. Because it was Sunday he could only stare at the telephone on the wall—too early to speak to anyone in New York, too soon to alert anyone in Los Angeles that he might be on his way. There was no one in Tokyo who could help him, either. His hand trembled as he poured the dark liquid into a cup. Helen was gone when he stepped back outside, blinking at the brightness after the dark of the kitchen. There was a sound, like a dove mewing. Coffee spilled over the rim of his cup.

"I've made a life for myself," she said as she deftly lifted the dripping cup from his hands. He was still blinking—in this chiaroscuro moment she seemed naked to him except for her breath and the scar.

"GO?" HE SAID. His throat—he had forgotten about it for a while, but it was still burning.

"Now."

She pulled the sheet up over her body and turned her face from him.

"Your husband's going to think it's really strange if he comes home and finds me gone."

"I'll handle it," she said. "He already thinks you're on the run."

"I'm not running," Danny said. "With the whole world wired, you can't really run anymore. So I'm walking. I'm walking."

"So walk."

"You're throwing me out?"

"You're going to Los Angeles."

"The whole point was coming here; I didn't want to get there."

"Take your time somewhere else then."

Danny sighed, and then the telephone rang.

Helen picked up the receiver. She said hello and then listened, said a few other things as Danny collected his clothes.

"It was Bar," she said when she hung up.

"I figured," Danny said, standing at the side of the bed where Helen lay fully exposed, the little half moon scar seeming almost decorative just above the wild black pubic thatch. Of a sudden he dropped to his knees alongside her, but she pushed his head away with the stiff thick base of her palm.

"Dress," she said.

"I'm getting dressed," he said, rising to his feet.

"You can write to me if you like."

"I'm not such a good correspondent. The telephone is my thing. And the fax."

"Then call. Fax. But don't ever show up again like this."

"Never?"

"No."

Danny stood there, waiting for something he could not figure, his raw throat pulsing, his legs as weak as reeds.

"Hey," he said, "I'm going. I just have to make a call."

"Call from the airport."

"I got to call a taxi."

"One call," she said.

"All right," he said, but he didn't move.

"Go," she said.

He walked to the door.

"Going."

In the doorway he turned, taking in the woman, the scar, the scattered bedclothes, the peculiar light in which all was momentarily suspended.

"Gone."

Dreamland

On the day Mike Quinn flew south for the first and last time he awoke in the grip of such hunger he thought he might be sick. But it was pure emptiness in his belly, he decided as he dressed for his quick trip to the office—he had just become a regional manager for a new software company out on Route 128—gobbling a jelly doughnut left over from a shopping trip he had taken over a week ago and washing the remains down with day-old coffee. Ever since he had moved out of the apartment, he had eaten on the run. Darcy, his wife of three years, had been the cook in the family.

"You treat me just like your mother, remember me telling you that?" she had said to him in one of the last rounds they had fought before splitting up this time. "Well, I'm not your mother, you know, and goddammit, I'm not even *related* to you so you had better start treating me like a human being or else you're not getting invited back."

He wondered as he dialed her number on a whim just before going out the door—was this treating her like a human being?

"Yeah?" a man said.

He hung up the telephone.

It rang just as he was picking up his suitcase.

"Hello?"

"Don't do that, Mike," Darcy said.

"Don't do what?"

"Call like that and hang up."

"I didn't call you."

"Mike, you can't fool me. I know you."

After a pause, he said, "Who was that?"

"A repairman."

"Sure."

"It was."

"Is he still there?"

"Yes."

"Let me talk to him."

"Mike, get out of here."

"I'm out," he said. "I'm going to Atlanta."

"You are?" There was some of the old excitement in her voice. "You got the job?"

"Yep."

"Congratulations. Oh, Mike, that'll really help you get off to a new start."

"A new start?"

"With your new life. Like we talked about."

"I got to go now," he said, his heart sinking like a heavy object in mud. Was this where treating her like a human being got him? He pictured a thick-necked, dark curly-haired repairman, his tools dangling from his wide belt, standing behind her, making nice with big fingers on her arms and chest.

"Come on, Michael," she said. "What good is talk if you don't follow through?"

"I'm following, okay?" he said. "I'm following." He hung up the telephone and went out the door. He climbed into his car and drove to the office where a small mound of paperwork remained to be dealt with, and then he drove to the airport where he parked his car and went to catch his airplane.

He did not have a lot of time before boarding—the row of telephone booths a few yards down the hall held his attention. Would it be treating her like a human being to call back and ask if they could see each other again when he returned from his trip? If he suggested that she might consider moving south with him when it came time to relocate? Soon he found himself sighing ferociously over the noise of the airplane engines at the lost opportunity to call her and ask.

"Are you okay?" asked his seat mate, a bony black woman in a navy blue suit who had been working in a lined notebook ever since they had taken off.

Quinn hadn't known many black people in his life, let alone black women who appeared to be employed by a company like his own. He began to speak, talking of business, and she spoke back, and soon they were going on about the coming election and it seemed that they could agree on a number of issues. Lunch was served. Not long after, they were preparing for their descent into the Atlanta area, as the soothing voice of the flight attendant informed them. And he had forgotten a lot of what had been on his mind.

The business in Atlanta kept him away from his troubles for the rest of the week. There was so much to do during the day, although Jack Henshaw, the big-handed, soft-voiced fellow who was his newly designated right-hand man, explained that in addition to everything else he was doing for Quinn he was also in charge of what he called "attitude adjustment."

"Things run a little slower down here," Henshaw said. "Not any worse, don't you worry about that. It's going to be as good as Boston, just . . ."— and here Henshaw smiled in a way that Quinn could have described as slyly. "See, Mike, it is Mike, isn't it? See, after your Yankee general Sherman left the city in ruins, we took us a while to look around and contemplate the mess. But we're rebuilding now. It's just a little more relaxed . . . than up your way."

By Wednesday, Quinn knew he could use some kind of adjustment. He decided that instead of calling it a night after one drink in the hotel bar he would suggest to Henshaw that they take a look at the town.

"Now what'd you have in mind?" Henshaw appeared to be studying him. "I mean, topless? That what you're thinking? Hell, I could do some of that. I haven't done it in a long time." He paused as Quinn shook his head. "Well, then, what else you got in mind?"

"Huh?" Quinn pursed his lips. "Nothing else. Sure, we could try a topless bar . . ."

"You're the boss," Henshaw said. "I'll just go and give the little woman a call and tell her to watch Johnny Carson without me tonight."

The little woman, Quinn was thinking, as he watched his companion walk slowly toward the telephones in the palm-infested lobby. He had been daring himself to call Darcy again. Maybe after another drink or two he might try it, but not now.

"Well, hell in a ball court," Hensaw said, catching Quinn in that thoughtful pose. "Look, I got to take a rain check on this carousing stuff tonight. Don't get started thinking that I'm pussy-whipped or anything like that, but seems like my older boy just got into a little fender-bender out near the interstate and I got to go and fetch him from the garage where he got towed."

"No, sure, I understand," Quinn said. "You got to go. I'm just going to finish this drink and head upstairs myself, anyway. See you tomorrow."

"Early in the morning, bright-eyed and bushy-tailed, I'll be there," Henshaw said.

Quinn watched him leave the bar in the direction of the exit to the street. As soon as he was gone, Quinn felt a sudden sadness overcome him, the common variety of sorrow that often descends on a traveler alone at night in a strange city. He wanted to get up and chase after Henshaw, tell him that he would help him find his son—he and Darcy had no children of their own and he was always curious about other people's offspring—and then perhaps have a drink with him and his wife at home. Instead he sat and had another drink alone, listening idly to the murmuring voices in the bar.

At around eleven o'clock he found himself yawning and left the bar. A flashing light from a passing police car caught his eye as he walked through the lobby, and he slowed down, then stopped. A large brick plaza lay beyond the revolving door. A taxi lingered there a moment, then pulled away. Quinn, as if drawn by a magnet, entered the revolving door and pushed and exited into the unexpected coolness of the night.

It's supposed to be warmer here than up north, he thought to himself as he walked across the hotel plaza to the near corner—Peachtree Street, Gone with the Wind, all that. There was a breeze, but he assured himself that he should not be surprised. He had done some reading about the territory. Atlanta was the highest American city east of Denver. So why not a breeze like this? He found himself walking south on Peachtree among high-rises and weedy lots with old wooden buildings falling in on themselves as if in despair at their own antiquity. At the far corner he saw a slender young thing in a miniskirt and skimpy blouse clinging to a lamppost as though it were a palm tree.

"Hi," the young thing said with a wink.

It was a boy's voice, tuned unnaturally high. Quinn pondered this on the short walk back to the hotel. It was midnight when he reached his room. Was the message light winking? Yes? No. He sat on the corner of the bed, studying the telephone, thinking, yes, I'll call her, no, I won't. He lay back to think about it, his exhaustion wrapped around him like a blanket.

Henshaw picked him up at eight-thirty, too alert and cheerful for Quinn's mood. Henshaw wasn't a stupid man, and as soon as he saw what he was dealing with he went quiet. Quinn was pleased. By noon, though, some of his old energy returned and Quinn suggested that they walk out for lunch. He told Henshaw about his stroll the night before, mentioning the transvestite.

"Hot-lanta," Henshaw said. "They come from all over the South to this place, doing their things. Though now AIDS is killing them off."

Quinn reached for something in his mind out of his college days. "It's like the Black Plague," he said as they stopped in front of a restaurant.

Henshaw laid a hand on his shoulder and leaned conspiratorially toward his ear. "Oh, we had *that* for years."

Later in the afternoon Henshaw appeared at his desk, all smiles. "Hey, you know I felt real bad having to leave you by yourself last night . . ."

Quinn shrugged. "Look . . ."

"No, no," Henshaw said. "I just talked to a buddy of mine . . . and we have a deal going for this weekend. He's got a little plane, my pal, Bobby . . . and some tickets for the game."

"The game?"

"YOU'RE WHAT?" DARCY said when he finally worked up the courage to call her. "A football game? I thought you hated football. Michael, maybe you're finding a new you down there. I'm happy for you."

"Oh, don't be happy for me," he said.

"Why shouldn't I?"

"Because it's condescending," he said, wondering where within himself he had found that word.

"You're the one who acted like I was your mother—"

"Oh, shut up," he said.

"Don't tell me to shut up."

"My mother is dead."

"Don't go pulling that number on—"

He touched a heavy finger to the bar on the receiver and her voice went away. Lying in the dark room he felt the sadness roll over him, as if he were a little boy once more and his mother had left him alone in the house while she went out to the corner store. It amazed Quinn just how far back in his life he could sink when pushed over into this feeling. Darcy—that woman! She had treated him as though he were the one who had stepped out of the marriage.

The pillow skidded out from under his head and he leaned down to retrieve it, feeling the sudden rush of blood to his brain. An hour later he was fending off a headache, obsessed once again, in spite of himself, with the recollection of Darcy's infidelity, the look on her face when he surprised her with his question, the telephone calls that he answered that awful week from the caller who clicked off each time he said hello—and her triumphant expression, a stay against guilt he understood if he considered it carefully, when she finally admitted she had done it. So it was one of those nights again, he assured himself, when he could stand for hours at the hotel window, as he was doing now, staring out across the city, pleased because he knew that other men in those apartment buildings and hotels and shanty rentals were suffering as he had, and even now some of them were discovering for the first time their capacity for betrayal, or the power of their shame. It was around one o'clock or so when Quinn turned from his observation post, went to the television, thought better of it, undressed, climbed into bed, and fell asleep.

THEY TOOK OFF from a small field north of the city, three men, their bags, a case of whiskey.

"Hot damn," Henshaw said, leaning forward to slap his friend the pilot on the shoulder. "You run out of fuel, we got enough of this good drink to fly us to China."

As if in response, the aircraft dipped its wings to the south and went into the wide curve that would point it toward their destination. Quinn's heart twitched—he had never flown in an airplane this small, and his fingers dug into his thighs as the raucous engine jerked them higher and higher through wispy clouds. For over an hour, Quinn's breathing seemed tuned to the noise of the machine, fading in and out as the whine rose and fell, and when they finally went into their descent toward the small orange-brown field below he pressed back against his seat, feeling the sweat pour down his sides. He had not paid much attention to Henshaw, who now seemed well on his way toward incomprehensibility, jibbering oddly, only now and then saying words that had something to do with football.

"Gol," said the man who had flown the airplane just as they came to a stop on the makeshift runway. He slapped his hand to his head and let out a gush of air from between his thick lips. "I ain't been that scared since I first started flying!" He reached under his jacket and came up with a flask he passed to Quinn. "How'd *you* like it?" Quinn noticed the smoke pouring out of the little panel in front of the controls.

So he had a few drinks himself on the way to the motel. It seemed in keeping with his retroactive fear for his life—and with the cars filled with fans of the Crimson Tide and of the Bulldogs, too, who flew pennants from their aerials, who waved pennants and pompoms and shot the bird at each other. Out on the strip where they took their rooms the motel lobby was jammed with more celebrants. It was far different from the way he had imagined such a scene, with some of the women and men dressed as if for a night at the theater and others in red hats and red shirts and red trousers, some even wearing red face-paint. Here and there he saw a black face or two, and though he was sure it was an illusion, he thought he might have seen the same trim black woman who had been his seat mate on the flight south.

"Bobby booked this room three months in advance, thank the Lord," Henshaw said, clear speech returning suddenly to him as they entered the hallway behind the lobby. Two bottles gone—he flipped the next one into the waste basket soon after they entered their room—and the game was still hours away.

"Bobby?" Quinn leaned against the wall and stared out the window at a patch of sky nearly white.

"Remember that boy flew us here?"

"Bobby?"

"That's the dog, bubba," Henshaw said.

"Dog?"

"Hey, y'all ready for murder and mayhem? We're going to whup their Alabama behinds!"

"Huh?" Quinn looked around. Henshaw stood in the bathroom door, his penis in hand, spraying urine across the rug. "Hey!"

"Haw, haw!" Henshaw made a funny laugh, looked down at his shoes and went back into the bathroom.

"Dum-da-dum-dum!" A loud thudding on the door. "Hey, y'all let us in!"

Bobby stared at Quinn when he yanked open the door. Much redder in the face than when he was last seen, Bobby had a young blond woman on each arm. "Gol," he said, "what's that stink?"

"Who's 'at?" Henshaw shouted from the bathroom.

"Santa Claus," Bobby said, motioning with his chin for Quinn to back up into the room so that he and the women could enter.

"It does stink," said one of the women, a short girl with a sweater that said BULLDOGS across her large chest. "Hi," she said, extending a hand toward Quinn. "I'm Tiffany."

"And I'm Brittany," said the other woman, who stood tall beside her companion but not in comparison to the men. She wore a red dress cut way above the knee.

It was Tiffany—or was it Brittany?—Quinn was so drunk he couldn't tell which girl was which—who pressed close to him in the rental car on the way to the stadium. "Are you a doctor?" she said.

"No," Quinn said, "do you need one?"

"Whooeee!" Henshaw kept yelling out the car window on the passenger's side of the wheel—Bobby, good old Bobby, was their pilot.

"I was going out with one," the girl said.

"Where's he?" Quinn said.

"He's dead," the girl said.

"I'm sorry," Quinn said.

"Oh, that's all right," the girl said. "I didn't know him real well."

"Oh?" Quinn felt her press harder against him, as though they were rounding a turn when they were still only pushing straight ahead along the road. "How'd he die?"

"His wife shot him," the girl said. "He was a real hero. She was trying to shoot me, I just know it, but he stepped in front."

"Dogs!" Henshaw shouted out the window. "Dogs! You 'Bama slime-buckets! Dogs!" He turned around and breathed fiery whiskey breath onto the rear seat passengers.

"Boston, you now an official Dog! You hear? You are an official Dog!"

"Arf," Quinn said. "Arf, arf!" The two girls giggled. He barked again.

Tiffany—or was it Brittany?—leaned over and gave him a big wet kiss on the cheek. It went like that all through the afternoon, the roaring smashing cheering game, the drinking, coughing, barking, shrieking Tiffany and Brittany, tens of thousands like them on both sides of the field, an enormously roaring blur of red and white and sky and green field, the ball soaring, clash of helmets and pads, the bottle in hand, empty, smashing, the feel of her next to him, singing the songs he never knew.

The ride back was louder, more drinking. The loss made them thirsty, hungry. Tiffany—or was it Brittany?—laid her head on Quinn's lap, nibbling now and then at his knee. Henshaw shouted at Bobby, foreign autos honked at them, Bobby honked back. When they reached the motel, Quinn got out and stood there awhile, waiting for the sun to go down. A car full of bearded men in camouflage pulled up next to him, idled there awhile, then drove off. The sun settled slowly down behind the restaurants and the tire store on the other side of the road.

"Let's go, you dirty defeated Dog," Henshaw said from behind him. Bobby came up on the other side of him with the girls in tow. They hustled him back into the automobile.

"Follow them," Henshaw said, and Quinn noticed that a car was leading them along the commercial strip.

"Can you believe it?" one of the girls said.

Along with the sweet odor of heavy perfume, there was a sour tinge of vomit in Quinn's nose.

"Sangwich," said one of them, Brittany or Tiffany.

"White bread, baloney, white bread," said Tiffany or Brittany, whacking him with her hip.

"Want to call home," Quinn heard himself say.

They were streaming along beneath dark trees, suddenly real country all around. Quinn wanted to close his eyes. Something purred in his lap— one of the girls, Tiffany or Brittany, was snoring, breathing with her mouth open on his knee.

Next thing, they were thrown forward as Bobby slammed on the brakes. Here they were—out in the woods somewhere—at a stucco-brick shack with a sign in neon glowing up top—

DREAMLAND

"Heard of this place?" Henshaw said.

"I told them," one of the girls said with a giggle.

"I did," the other girl said.

A few couples huddled outside the door. Inside it was all dim neon and the smell of the wood oven and the odor of roasting meat and pungent sauce. It took a long time before they got a table, and they drank beer all that while. When they finally sat down Quinn felt as though he were sinking into a bath of beer. People raised slabs of animal ribs to their mouths, or bottles of beer, or both. Most of the diners were white, but all of the crew behind the counter, the huge man sitting at the roasting pit, the people in the grease-stained photographs on the walls—except for a pale-faced old man whom Quinn knew he should know but couldn't name—all were black.

Quinn felt the girl's hip —Tiffany's or Brittany's?—bumping against him as she chewed her meat. The sauce stuck to his fingers. His face was smeared with grease from the bones he gnawed on. More beer. And more beer. He had such a sensation in his mouth from the hot sauce, in his chest, in his limbs from all the drinking, that for a moment he looked around, beyond the tables to the counter, and had a fearful insight—that he was biting directly into and chewing on the barbecued flesh of the black men behind the barriers.

"Do we know how to party here, sugar?" one of the girls said to him.

"Aw," Henshaw said, "y'all come to Hot-lanta, we'll show you—"

Quinn was feeling queasy. Seeing Bobby take a slice of white bread from the plate in the middle of the table and wipe his lips, he did the same. And then he stood up. Something was calling him, and it was more than his kidneys and bladder, though God knew these organs were bleating out distress signals. The call took him to the door.

Men and girls. More of them milling about outside the entrance. Cars roared up, cars departed. Quinn wandered off toward the trees. A little wind blew up, but not cold. He leaned against a tree, as if he were waiting for someone to come by. Lights from a van caught him turning back toward the roadhouse. No one seemed to be left in front—or the lights blinded him to their presence.

"Hey," came a voice from the van. "You one of the Thetas?"

Quinn was shaking his head when two young men appeared on either side of him and herded him toward the van.

"Tour is leaving," one of them said. There was an odor about the vehicle, Quinn noticed, when he climbed in and sat on a jump seat among a half dozen other travelers. Barbecue sauce—perfume that might have been Brittany's or Tiffany's—beer. Mostly it was his own smell, the odor of others around him, these young boys and girls, swaying from side to side as they drove along narrow country roads, that weighed him down where he sat, swaying along with the passage of the van.

"Well-fed, well-drunk," someone said at his ear.

"Now the rest," said another.

"Rest is best," another said.

"Hey, you're a poet and you don't even know it."

"Off to Moundsville," said a boy at his back. Except that Quinn understood it as "Mow-nnds-veel . . ."

He dozed, awoke to the sound of the Theta boys singing, joking. Glasses clinked, bottles clacked together. Was it twenty minutes it took them? More? Suddenly the van jolted across railroad tracks, made a sharp turn, stopped abruptly. Where'd my friends go? Quinn said to himself, sitting up nearly alert. If they are my friends. Someone got out and left the door open. Cool breeze filtered through the van. Moans. Groans.

"I have to get going," Quinn said but no one seemed to be listening. He slumped down into himself, wondering at his own stupor.

"I need a ride," he said.

"You're riding," a boy said in the dimness that enfolded them.

Suddenly the door slammed and they were moving again. Then stopped. And then moved again. Then stopped. Someone yanked open the rear door. Quinn piled out with the rest, these college boys and a few girls.

Tall mounds surrounded them in the moonlight, strange hills in this flat country that seemed, when he noticed it, arranged as if by the hands of some giant's child across the grassland of this park. Following the group, he made a telephone call in his mind, saying to her, You wouldn't believe it, Dar—and in the same exchange she cut him off with a snarling, You bastard, sneaking around with those co-eds, huh? Well—

It wasn't like that. No one paid any attention to him, even passing a bottle over to him without looking him in the eye. It was as though he were a chaperone, an almost invisible one at that, or something like a ghost. The drink made him feel real, though, and he drank another, tasting grease on his lips, the lingering traces of the barbecue where for the moment he had imagined they had been eating the roasted flesh of negroes—and wiping his face with the white skin of young girls.

I'm an adult, a manager, I shouldn't be thinking like this, I shouldn't even be here, he said to himself as he trekked across the park.

"Talbot has the key," someone said up ahead of him.

"Talbot has the key," the group took up the chant.

"Hey," Quinn said, catching up with the last boy in the line ahead of him.

"Arf, arf," the boy said.

"Y'all coming?" a girl called over her shoulder.

It was a bright night full of moon. From the top of the mound—a broad grassy space large enough, it appeared, to capture that moon high above if it happened to fall right now—he could see the long row of strange hillocks.

"Who made all these?" he said.

"Arf, arf," said the boy next to him.

"Injins," came an answer in the voice of a sleepy young girl.

Someone handed him a bottle.

"Black warriors," said another.

"Asshole, that's just a river," someone else put in.

"No, no, hey, dey be de black warriors, wid de black faces . . ."

"Talbot?" someone called out.

Talbot had the key. Quinn took a sharp hot swallow from the bottle and followed the wavery line of students down the slope toward a low building on the far side of a mound. A blond-haired fellow—Talbot?—worked at the lock, and then suddenly the door swung open.

"*Museum* . . ." was all Quinn noticed about the sign in the dark before he entered along with the noisy knot of students. Inside, someone found a light switch, and the entire place came up brightly, filled with cases along the wall showing pottery and maps and in one room a little exhibit filled with life-sized models of Indians at their fire.

"Talbot's daddy's an anthomologist," said a red-faced girl at his side. "He runs this place." She tugged at his sleeve. "Come and see."

They wandered away from the main room, the sounds of the other partygoers fading, echoing, fading in and out, faintly, bouncing off the walls. Quinn's bowels cried out to him suddenly with a burning and a twisting that made him stop, take a deep breath.

"I got to . . ."

"What's that?" the girl said, looking back over her shoulder. Her dress swayed, her hips.

"What's your name?"

"What's yours?" she said.

"Tal . . . bot . . ." came a faint cry from far away.

"Tal . . ."

". . . bot . . ."

"Can I have some?" the girl said, stepping close to him. Her hair smelled wonderful, but her breath was foul. Her eyes lighted up, and then seemed to darken.

"What?" Quinn said.

"Whatever you brought," she said.

They heard voices approaching. Lights in the other rooms blinked on and off. Someone barked like a dog. Quinn backed up against a railing.

"You got to get something," the girl said as she pressed herself against him.

He twisted around, fearful that she might breathe on him again. Her face—so much like either Britanny's or Tiffany's—seemed to glow with the curious light of the deep sea when, as he had once read, tens of hundreds of millions of microscopic animals float on the waves beneath the moon. His mouth hurt, as though by mistake he had bitten into something too hard for his teeth. He could taste blood, mixed with the sour traces of alcohol. In his mind he found the telephone, picked it up, dialed Darcy's number, *mis*dialed, tried again, heard the ringing at the other end of the line.

A crash of glass distracted him

"Down there," said the girl, pushing him toward the railing.

"Where?"

"There," she said again, pointing down into the pit that seemed just to have opened, though it must always have been there.

It was a burial pit, at the bottom of which lay several carefully arranged skeletons of the Indians who built the mounds many hundreds of years ago—how many fucking hundred? someone was saying as the crowd of fraternity revelers now gathered at the railing, tossing bottles, some empty, some full, into the abyss.

"Nonononononononono my Daddy'll—" a boy was shouting.

"Help him," the girl said, meaning for Quinn to hold another boy's legs while he tottered high above on the railing and urinated into the pit.

Quinn held him tight, responding with his grip to the screams of joy and fear around him. A resiny mist settled on his lips. He looked up and leaned around—the boy's face was a mask of bulging eyes and clenched teeth—and then he let go.

An Afternoon of Harp Music in Lake Charles, Louisiana

All day it went back and forth from brutality to boredom. Louise, her mind already on the weekend and the questions it raised, put forward her figures and each time this one bully—full red face, his eyes red, too, as though he had brushed his teeth with bourbon, and wearing an expensive blue-and-white-striped shirt and black suspenders—carped at her throughout her presentation.

"Are you certain?" he said, staring at her in a way so raw that you would have thought that his partners were not seated in the same room.

"Let me put it this way," Louise said, as though she were speaking to someone for whom English was a second language. "I have all the figures right here, and I'll check the computations for you again if you like." She whipped out her calculator from her attache case and sat poised, ready once again to do the numbers. She could feel the tickle of sweat running down her sides, trickling all the way down past the waistband of her pantyhose.

This was a system worth millions, and she was selling it—sold it to them already, but had to play out the game plan, just as she had been doing for years—and after she recalculated a second time by another method and showed the men the results, the red-faced partner seemed to have lost interest in her. In fact, he was the one who just before lunch stood up and announced that they should all just get on with it and let her prep the office manager.

Maybe he's on medication, Louise considered as she watched him amble from the room while several of the other men lingered to go over a few of the details one more time.

One of them asked her to dinner, but she declined, explaining that she was driving over to Louisiana the next morning to spend the weekend with her twin sister whom she hadn't seen in years and wanted to do a little shopping for a house present for her.

"See my secretary on your way out," the man said. "She'll help you with it."

"You know what you want to get her?" the girl asked when Louise told her of her quest. She had pretty eyes, penciled in dark like those on a movie-star doll, and a sparkling engagement ring on her finger.

"Only vaguely," Louise said.

"Go to the Galleria," the girl said. "It's got millions of shops, right down from your hotel."

The hotel: she went there first, in a cab that swung up to the curb the moment she left the cool interior of the office building for the plaza before it—it was June and this was Texas, so there was already enough humidity in the air to drench a rug. Riding in the back of the disinfectant-soaked taxi, she felt the familiar sense of relief that came at the end of a school day years and years ago. The worst was over. One short follow-up session on Monday with the technical personnel and that was that. Another feather—with dollar signs dangling from it—in her little cap.

Stepping into her room and seeing the red message light blinking on the telephone, her heart leaped like a five-year-old's. And then her hope caved in when she heard the message.

"You still going to the Galleria?" the painted secretary asked when Louise called back.

"I am."

"Good, because I just remembered the cutest store . . ." And she proceeded to give Louise the location, second level, near the ice-skating rink.

"Ice-skating?"

"Wait'll you see it," the secretary said.

"Thank you," Louise said, realizing that this was Texas and that Texans seemed to want you to feel so much at home that you never left, an attractive thought when you considered what some people—me, she admitted—had to go back to. Minneapolis. An apartment with some plants and cats in whose company she sometimes felt excluded.

I should welcome this heat, she told herself as she set out for the Galleria. The moment she left the hotel lobby she knew it was a mistake to walk. Nobody except the poor and the mad walked in this city, if it *was* a city, instead of a collection of interlocking malls and subdivisions and highways and office complexes, with some vacant lots between. Sleek new cars passed her along the way, only the diesels among them making much of a sound. She had rented a red Pontiac at the airport. Why had she left it in the hotel garage? Halfway to her destination, she felt as though she might melt into a pool of sweat. The sun was hidden behind the tall office towers, though its egg-yolk orange light reflected off the large windows of buildings to the east and its heat remained unabated. A hot lazy wind blew past her carrying the odors of automobile exhaust, steamy metal, and the faint hint of spicy cooking. For a light-headed moment Louise feared that she might somehow get lifted on this wind and carried up toward the glass windows behind which sat pig-eyed, beefy-cheeked men and their secretaries, with their bouffant hairdos, ready to serve them.

Past a fountain and up the triple decks of cement terraces, she entered the huge air-conditioned mall. A few quick shivers and it was as if she had never been hot. Immediately she found herself immersed in a wide stream of shoppers coming up on elevators, or down, most of them women of all ages—the fat chub of a child in her mother's arms, an elderly, nearly bald woman in a fashionable jump suit, from the sleeves of which her arms stuck out like those of a scarecrow. Louise had to look twice, the resemblance to her mother was so uncanny. As she took the moving stairs to the next level, she glanced back for another glimpse of the ancient shopper, but the woman had faded into the crowd.

Ice skaters in June! The sight of them edged from her mind any other thoughts. Skimming, whirling skaters! Some girls, some boys, a few women, slicing around and around the wide oval rink while piped-in music—flabby pop-rock—flowed over their heads. The skaters, the shoppers, the music, the cool air—cool but not icy enough to make her shiver any more after her initial shock—all this gave her such a sudden feeling of vertigo that Louise might have been coming out of a spin on the ice. Clasping a hand on the rail, she closed her eyes and tried to clear her head.

"Oil did it all," came a voice at her ear.

She turned to see the red-faced, beefy-cheeked lawyer.

"What are you doing here?" she said.

He opened his eyes wider than he had at any moment during their meeting. Now she could actually see their color—a sharp, piercing blue.

"I live here. Not in this mall, I mean, but in this town. Why shouldn't I be here?"

"Did you follow me?"

He flicked a look at the skaters, then back to her. A sound came out of his mouth, the kind of noise that worries you when you make it yourself.

"I . . ."

"You did, didn't you?"

Despite the crowds of shoppers, the dozens of skaters skimming across the ice, a strange feeling of intimacy overtook her. Louise felt as though it were just the two of them, compacted together into a small space, as in a movie closeup, the air around them reduced, just enough for taking quick, shallow breaths.

"You were really nasty to me in that meeting. Did you follow me so you could apologize?"

"You might could put it that way," the lawyer said.

"So you *did* follow me?"

"I . . . learned of your destination." He shrugged, and held up his hands as though to scrutinize them in special light.

"Why did you give me such a hard time?"

He lowered his head a little, which gave him the appearance of a boy trying to show remorse. "I don't know what got into me."

"You made my morning difficult."

"Sorry," he said.

"Apology accepted," she said, thinking that it really wasn't all right, but that she still had to work with him and his group on Monday.

"So you'll come out?"

"Out where?"

"Out to the ranch."

"What are you talking about?"

He raised his head, stood to full height. "I'd like you to come out to the ranch and have supper with me."

Louise shook her head. "I don't think so." Adding, "Thank you very much."

"It's just . . ."

"Just what?"

She sighed and shook her head. It was incredible, to be standing here and talking to this stranger—a mean bastard, to boot—as though they had been held together for years by stupid affection and sorrows of one kind or another.

"I've got to buy something," she said, and rushed away blindly into the nearest shop while he stood waiting for her to return.

"Let's get out of here," he said when she got back. "Watching these folks on the ice makes me thirsty. You thirsty?"

The chill of this enclosed space, and now the warmth of suddenly rising blood on her chest and cheeks, it all conspired to make her say yes. And in the hesitant moment in which she admitted this to herself, the red-faced lawyer moved close to her and bumped his shoulder—gently, surprisingly for a man of his bulk—against her, as though he were the leader of a herd of some large land animals, or even a creature of the sea, and was ordering her with his gesture to make a certain turn.

"Where?" she said, moving with him toward the elevator.

"Well, it doesn't have to be the ranch, we can find a place around here."

"There's a bar in my hotel," she said.

"Well, let's go," he said. "I'll follow you over."

"I walked," she said. "It's not far."

"Nobody walks outside here," he said.

"I did."

"I have a phone in the car."

"You do?"

"Yeah."

"What's that got to do with anything?"

"I'm going to call the *Chronicle*. 'Out-of-town woman walks to Galleria.' I can see the headlines in tomorrow's paper."

"That's what passes for news around here?"

"Well," he said, pointing to the elevator, "I didn't add the rest of it. Too horrible."

The elevator door slid open and closed after them. He pushed a button and then they descended.

"Which is?"

"Woman walks to Galleria, meets murderer at curbside."

"Is that what happens to people who walk around here?"

"At least once a month."

The elevator door slid open again, revealing the parking garage. She walked with him, giving in for a few seconds to a childish fantasy—that he was one of those killers and had stalked her and now was taking her to his car so he could drive her to some far-off place and do the deed—and then shaking it off, with a little warning to herself. Not about murder, but about sex.

In the car—low, black, streamlined, leather seats, leather dash—she started to tell him where she was staying but he cut her off.

"I know," he said.

"You've done your research."

"It's a small world, over in our office."

They passed a uniformed guard leaning against a pillar, watching their passage.

"Dangerous in here, too?"

"It happens," he said.

He spun the car up the circling ramp and out into the bright sun. Louise blinked hard, her eyes adjusting to the light. She covered them with her hands, feeling the cool gust of air blowing from the dash. He steered them onto the street, turning south toward her hotel. While he concentrated on the business of the road, she let her hands drop and sneaked her first real look at him. Minus the sneering smile, he didn't seem all that repulsive. And his hands looked good gripping the wheel, and she watched—just for a fleeting second—the way his legs moved as he adjusted the speed and then caught the brake to slow down at a stop sign.

IT HAD BEEN years since she had had so much to drink. And it had been—she knew the exact figure—four years since she had let a man into her bedroom, let alone a man for whom she had felt so much anger and distrust. If she hadn't known better, she would have thought that he had somehow hypnotized her. But she knew this was all her own doing. If she didn't want *him*, she wanted *this*. It was ridiculous, but she was caught up in it now, unable to remember his name but admiring the way he lowered his suspenders with a graceful, almost mimelike motion, to let them dangle below his waist like some strange apparatus that might have belonged to his body and then again might not. She caressed his striped trousers, enjoying the feel of the rich fabric beneath her fingers, undoing the fly and grasping his distended member, red as his face that morning, and opening her jaws wide—picturing a snake, of all convoluted things to think about, taking in a frog, and she laughed down in her throat and through the haze of the vodka she heard him say, "Funny?"

And then she was back on her feet, pushing him back down on the bed, climbing up and squatting over him.

"Whoa," he said.

"Too late," she said, pressing her knees against his arms.

"Yeow!" he cried out like a little boy in pain.

"What are you doing?"

"Right now? Being attacked!"

"No, I mean, following me, getting me drunk."

"What am I doing? Just what you think."

"No, what? You trying to get me to drop the price for the system, is that it?"

"Oh, man," he said, narrowing his eyes as he stared up at her, "you Yankees are paranoid. Drop the price? I don't care about the price. I'll get them to double the amount. Hell, I was just looking for some company."

"I'm not a Yankee," she said, Her heart was beating fast, and with the taste of him in her mouth it was difficult—she could admit this to herself—to stay calm. A certain kind of moment had passed, but another had arrived.

"You talk like one."

"I'm from Knoxville," she said. "I went to business school in Pennsylvania. That's what you hear. I lost my drawl."

"I went to school up in Cambridge, Massachusetts. How come it didn't touch my drawl?"

Louise rolled to one side, sprawling next to him on the bed without touching.

"Where'd you get your strength?" he said, twisting around to speak.

"I'm on the road a lot," she said. "I work out.

"So you're the modern liberated woman, huh? My ex—she was a cave woman. Nothing modern about her except her car and her car phone and her lawyer." He was breathing easily—she was listening carefully—and suddenly he took a deep breath and then spoke again. "So, are you attached to somebody at the end of the road?"

"I used to be, but not anymore."

The broad space of sky outside the hotel room window turned from peach to lavender to bruise-purple, then black. This space of color and light remained the pivot point on which the room, and the time, seemed to turn—everything moved except the spot where Louise fixed her eyes, her body spinning, the man above her whirling, the room tilting. Then he was gone, leaving her behind in a twist of damp and salty sheets.

But without dreams. She would, if asked, have described herself as usually a heavy dreamer, but this time she didn't dream. She went out like a spent light bulb. And when she awoke she could tell by something in the air that she had slept long and hard. The sex had doped her. She had forgotten how potent a drug it could be. She had forgotten how when she awoke from the sleep it induced she felt as though the world had been emptied of everything except her sense of loss.

SHE DRESSED IN a rush, anxious to get on the road. It took her until the turn onto Interstate 10 East before she began to wonder seriously why the lawyer hadn't called to say thank you and good morning. Texans were usually hospitable, yes?

It didn't matter, though, she told herself, driving long and hard, past flooded fields and vast patterns of oil rigs and refinery towers laced against the sky. Between Houston and Beaumont smokestacks, the thick dark clouds of waste floating above the fields. In this part of the world at this time of year it always seemed as though it might rain. In this corner of the state, it seemed as though the rain might fall as acid, eating into your vehicle, perhaps even into your skin.

A dark gray-black cloud stretched above her like an old umbrella when she pulled into a truck stop. In the rank stall where she yanked down her pants, she had to admit that the sensation of his presence was palpable. This soreness was a souvenir, after all. And what if?

But who worried about infection for more than a fleeting second? Sermonizers, and the unlucky. For now, she could remember, and the memory meant something beyond the stinging in her flesh.

"LINDY?"

She spoke into the telephone, glancing around blankly at the inside of the crowded diner. Truckers, mostly, sat at the counters and stuffed the booths with their bulk and filled the air with cigarette smoke and the twangy jabber of their voices. No one like herself here—she'd have to travel a little while longer to see herself.

"I been worried sick," her sister said at the other end of the line.

"Not to worry," Louise said. "I'm on the way. On the interstate. Maybe an hour and a half away, not much more than that."

"Hurry up then." A familiar pause in the familiar voice. Lindy would be touching her tongue to the inside of her cheek. An old tic. "Be careful."

Louise made a sound to show her gratitude and they ended the conversation, and in her own arms and hands she felt the very movement Lindy was making a hundred or so miles down the road, the blessing and the curse of having this special sister. Peering through the smoke, Louise caught a glimpse of herself reflected in the glass behind the counter, and she pictured Lindy looking in a mirror and thinking the same thing to herself. It had been years since they had looked at each other directly, and Louise was wondering now if the visit was such a good idea after all.

Back in the car, she was caught up in the pulse and details of their long and entangled story when a long double-hitch trailer roared past her in the left lane, shaking her from her reverie. Louise looked out at its departing length, saw a bridge, and then a sign posted at the side of the road:

LOST AND OLD RIVERS

Do such things happen in life? They do, they do, here's the evidence! She turned quickly as if to verify that the sign was not an illusion as she rolled across the swampy, overflowing banks of what must be this double-named waterway. What a name! The name! Like a poem! A sign! A sign that's really a sign! Louise allowed herself a little pleasure, toying with the possibilities. Oh, God, to be a twin and an English major! What a fate! In a story, Louise decided, it would be at this point that the narrative rolled back in time to some of the earliest moments of her life together with Lindy. Lost and old rivers! Their mirrored days, how their father all too often confused one with the other, their mother's drunken rages, her own first love and Lindy's jealousy. She remembered being six years old, eight, fifteen, and then her twenties, and now this decade, all of it as run-together as the low tree line of the Louisiana countryside. Maybe that's why she didn't read much or go to movies anymore. She wanted things to be real—as real as this road, as real as this trip to see her sister after a five-year hiatus, to meet her new husband, to see how life might have turned out for her if Alex hadn't left. A house, a job that kept you in one place, quiet long hours together.

LAKE CHARLES

the sign came up, high clouds floating above. Only a few miles to go. A far cry from their old home, this swampy country. (And now she was making a little movie in her head.) Their father had come over the mountains from North Carolina, met their mother at a church social in Knoxville, married her, made his career in the biology department at the university. Those years flew past—and out of all of them what did she remember clearly? A flood in the basement of their house, wading through the water with Lindy, showing up for dinner with leeches clinging to their legs. A spanking. A door she had pushed open only to find her mother lying naked, weeping, on the bed, a cigarette burning in the ashtray—neither of her parents ever smoked—and the strange voice of a preacher on the radio. Father moving out and then coming around every weekend to take them to the mountains, sometimes to the mall. She had lived for her sister and her sister had lived for her.

It wasn't until she met Alex that she understood that she was supposed to live for herself first. His bearded cheeks, his hairless head, the low growl of his voice, big shoulders, the way he slouched and stared at her when they first met. Five years of her life she had spent with him, and how could you put that time back together? And who would want to? To reconstruct it would only bring back the pain. She had preferred years of work and abstinence to the torture of giving herself to someone who cared nothing for how much she might be worth.

Other memories came to mind as she drove the last part of the journey. Her father standing in a streambed, the water rushing past his naked calves, lapping at the uprolled cloth of his khaki trousers. That look in his blue eyes—*Come in*, it said, *come in*. But she hadn't. Too scared of the cold stream, and how old was she then? If only she'd dared. But I'm in now, she said, spying the turnoff. *I'm in.*

Following Lindy's directions, she found the street without much difficulty. Just as she had said in her letter, there was the large oak with the hanging moss that made up a curtain in front of the brown-shingled house. The heat here was intense and liquid, Louise noticed, as she left the car and walked beneath the curtain of moss. Above the town thunderheads gathered, the kind you usually saw only at a distance in Texas. Things were smaller here, the effects of nature more concentrated. I just hope that doesn't mean we're going to have a blowup, Louise said to herself. Given all that had happened in the last twelve hours, she didn't know if she was ready for it.

"You're here!" Lindy stood waiting for her at the front door.

Louise stopped, blinked at the sight of her. Everyone always said while they were growing up how it must be just like looking in the mirror. But it wasn't that way at all. Seeing her sister there on the step, it was like seeing herself—not in the mirror, but in some interior vision that made a glowing figure illuminated by the electricity of her own blood. Lindy's hair was different—hanging straight to her shoulders instead of Louise's businesslike feather cut—but in the sly look in her arched left eye, the way she clasped her hands in front of her, Louise saw herself for the first time since their separation.

"I'm here," she said, remembering to hand over the little gift.

"Well, come on in and meet everybody," Lindy said, taking the package from her and leaning forward to give her a kiss on the cheek.

That gravelly voice—Louise loved to listen to it, intrigued by the sound she knew must be the same tenor as her own. And on top of this she loved the thought that Lindy heard her voice in the same way. And sniffed her familiar scent in the same way.

"Who's 'everybody'?"

"A man, a child, a dog—fish."

"A child?"

"Harry's," her sister said, standing back from the doorway.

Inside the house ran a long hall, dark and damp, smelling of spices Louise couldn't name, and a hint of something else, something dank, as if the place had been flooded or buried and then readmitted to the world above water. Photographs on the wall showed stark stone cliffs and battlements below a grainy sky of clouds thick with storm. Cold in that world compared to the humid air she waded through here, the kind of hot damp that Houston only flirted with.

"Interesting pictures."

"Harry made them," Lindy said, setting the unopened package on a nearby table.

"You never mentioned the child to me," Louise said.

"He just came this year," Lindy said. "His mother . . . wanted a vacation."

"Just like our mother."

"Actually, something similar. But this is drugs, not booze."

"Much more expensive habit."

"Depends on how you calculate," Lindy said. She smiled, and said, "*Natchy?*"

"*Pooldoubly,*" Louise said, lapsing without a second thought into their old secret language.

"*Atcha outabee der offaback eh chum Harry.*"

"*Bin,*" Louise said.

"Okay," Lindy said, and Louise could almost hear the little *click* of release as they moved back into English.

Harry was kneeling at the side of a small pool in the center of the walled garden behind the house and looked up but didn't stand when the sisters walked out through the rear door. He was a husky blond man who seemed about their own age until you noticed the way his light hair blended into patches of silver at his temples. His eyes were an odd shade of green and Louise squinted at him, trying to figure the precise color.

"Hullo," he said in an accent that could have been Scottish or northern English.

"Hi," Louise said. "I'm the twin."

"I'm Harry," he said. "Just a second then." He leaned over the pool, peering down into the water.

"Oh," Louise said, catching a glimpse of a gold fin turning beneath the green murk.

"Golden carp," Harry said without looking up.

"Beautiful." Louise caught sight of another fish, this one as large as her forearm, turning at the edge of the underwater wall.

"Harry has nice hobbies," Lindy said.

"To compensate for terrible everyday work," Harry said, standing, finally, and with a smile offering his hand in greeting. "Pleased to meet you. Watch it, though, it's mucky."

Louise ignored his warning, took his wet hand in hers. A fetid odor rose from the pool behind him.

"So, Lindy told me you're working in Houston?"

"Just this week," she said. "I travel a lot. My territory is quite large."

"You're kind of a new twist on the old traveling salesman, then?" A little spark danced in Harry's eye.

It was one of those moments, and she never knew what to say. A splash at her feet—she glanced down at the disappearing fin of one of the carp. Saved by a fish!

Lindy, apparently oblivious to the way Harry had looked at her sister, led Louise back into the house and he followed after. Lunch was spicy crawfish bisque Lindy explained she had learned to prepare after years of living in Cajun country. Then came golden catfish fillets, blackened potatoes, and a salad; all of this they washed down with gallons of iced tea. If only Harry hadn't fixed his eyes on her throughout the entire meal!

"Tell me about your work," he said.

Louise talked about her company, the equipment, the route she managed.

"Too technical for me," Harry said.

"I was always the artist in the family," Lindy said. "I'd be practicing my flute and Daddy would take Louise up to his workshop and show her all these technical things. Never in a million years could I understand them. See," she said, picking at her food, "we're exactly alike and different as anything."

"It's just a knack I have," Louise said. "You've got your music—you still play, don't you? And I've got my mechanical skills. We're not that much different, no matter how hard we try to be."

Harry was shaking his head.

"I can't keep my eyes off you. Your voices are almost exactly alike. The way you both smile, the lifelines, the creases—"

"Please," Lindy said, staring at Louise, "no talk about lines and creases."

The telephone rang in another room and Harry stood up. "I know it's for me."

"Danny," Lindy said. "His son."

"He'll be wanting to come home," Harry said as he left the room.

"A nice boy," Lindy said. "For a teenager. He's very considerate. But Harry's worried that the boy's becoming too American."

"Where are they from?"

"Cardiff. A big old Welsh seaport."

"A long way from here," Louise said.

"Shorter than the distance from Minneapolis to Lake Charles," Lindy said.

"I'm overdue, I know," Louise said.

"I would have come to see you," Lindy said, "but—"

"I'm more mobile," Louise said. "Since Alex and I separated, at least. Five years is too long. I should have come sooner. I'm sorry. I'm sorry I didn't come sooner."

"I missed you," Lindy said.

"But with Harry and the boy—and the fish—you're not at a loss for company."

Lindy straightened her back and gave a little shake, like an animal trying to dry itself after a long dip in the pond. "There's someone else, too."

"What?"

Louise stared as a single tear, tiny as a pearl, appeared in the corner of her sister's left eye.

A door slammed in another part of the house and both women looked around.

"They're back," Lindy said. "We'll talk later."

"Wait," Louise said as Harry and the boy came into the room.

"Look what he's got," Harry said.

The boy held up a large dripping mass of shell.

"What is it?" Louise leaned forward.

"A turtle," the boy said.

Louise looked down at the mess on the carpet.

"Now we've got a problem," Harry said, "about where to keep this beast."

The boy looked at his father. "In the pond, sir," he said.

"It will eat the carp," Harry said.

"No, it won't," the boy said.

"Don't be stupid," Harry said. "Of course it will."

"Well, I don't care," the boy said.

"Put it in a box in the shed and we'll figure it out," Lindy said.

"What do you think?" Harry looked at Louise.

"What do I know about things like that? I'm just a visitor."

"Who *is* she?" the boy said.

"Your Aunt Louise?" Harry scowled at his son. "You can't tell? She looks exactly like your stepmother."

"No, she doesn't," the boy said.

"You're the first one ever to think so," Louise said.

"So?" The boy dangled the turtle, beak first, toward the already wet carpet.

"Where'd you find it?" Louise said.

"Didn't *find* it," the boy said. "We went hunting."

"Watch that surly tone now, lad," Harry said.

"Did you go hunting in the swamp?" Louise said.

"It's called a bayou here," the boy said.

"Be civil now," Harry said.

"So, in the bayou."

The boy nodded. "My buddies and I caught it."

"Then put the beast out in the shed as your mother suggested, Daniel," Harry said.

"My stepmother," the boy said.

"Go on," Harry said.

"Yes, sir," the boy said, going to the rear of the house, the turtle still dangling from his hand.

"So now you've met the whole family," Lindy said.

"Perhaps we can fix some tea then?" Harry said. "Come." He led Louise past her sister through several musty rooms to a screened-in porch that jutted out from the side of the house. It was damp here, too, with only the slightest wind stirring. He disappeared for a moment and then returned hauling a large golden instrument.

"Don't normally keep it out here," he said. "Too much moisture. But then there's scarcely a place where you don't find too much moisture in this town."

"You play?" Louise stared at the instrument.

"One of my many talents," Harry said, an odd smile passing across his face.

"I've never seen a man play a harp before," Louise said.

Lindy stepped into the room. "He's an unusual man," she said.

"The way the joke goes," Harry said, "I'm practicing to be an angel." He pulled the instrument onto a stand in front of a large easy chair and commenced to tune the strings. "Though one should never add things up until all the figures are in, should one?"

"What do you mean by that?" Lindy threw herself down on the sofa next to Louise and folded her arms across her chest.

Harry shrugged, still working at the strings, the pretty, if monotonous, plucking at the scale.

"Now you've got a surprise for your sister, haven't you?"

"I've been waiting to hear," Louise said, sitting up.

"It's a tune of O'Carolan's," Harry said. "We've been rehearsing." His hands flowed in an oblate trajectory before him, on either side of the harp strings, while Lindy, standing, reached behind her and produced a flute.

"Is this what you wanted to tell me?" Louise said.

Her eyes half-closed as she swayed to the sinuous melody, Lindy gave her sister a shake of the head. The flowing waves of the harp strings settled Louise back in her seat while the line on the flute carried her up and over the house in her thoughts, over the trees all around, the water everywhere, too, and all of it connected somehow to the stream she had recalled on the drive over, her father's bare calves, trouser legs damp from the rushing flow.

What was her sister's news? She wondered as she watched and listened, Harry's fingers plucking at the strings as though he were seated at a loom weaving, Lindy's puckered lips nearly touching the metal mouthpiece but not quite. Louise herself had never been musical and so Lindy's talent had always intrigued her—there was this difference between them almost from the start.

And there was something else and she would hear her sister's secret soon, though she wasn't sure it would make any difference in the way she was feeling. It used to be that having Lindy in her life made things seem balanced and comprehensible. But seeing her this time after so long an absence was having the opposite effect from what she had anticipated— not order, but fear bordering on chaos, unless it was true, as she had felt more and more, that fear ordered things as much as hope.

But then she got caught up in the music again, the lifting, lofting melody, and the reassuring buoyancy of the flowing rhythms, the strings, the flute, and she soared with it, giving herself over to the passing attraction of form—amazed that it came from this man with such an odd manner and from her sister's lips, lips identical to hers but oh, so different! The years of needless separation, her indolence and her meanspirited desire to stay away from this mirror image of herself who seemed, even in her fears and ignorance, everything Louise desired to become—all the time they might have spent together that had flowed away into lost and old rivers rushing back to her, and it became difficult to catch her breath.

"So beautiful," she said when she could speak again.

Lindy merely stared at her, laying down her instrument while Harry, caught in the final runs of another old tune, swept his hands across the resonating strings.

"Did you enjoy it?" Lindy touched a hand to her sister's cheek.

"It was so beautiful," Louise said again. And then in their private language she said to her sister, *"What is your secret?"*

Lindy shook her head. *"Secret?"*

"You said there was someone else."

"Oh," Lindy said, in a slightly embarrassed voice. *"It's nothing."*

"What do you mean?" She looked over at Harry, who seemed both puzzled and pleased to hear them jabber in their special tongue. *"Is it him? Is there something about him?"*

"*Oh, no,*" Lindy said. "*It's something else.*"

"*What are you talking about? Are you having an affair?*"

"*You might say I've found someone,*" Lindy said.

"*Oh, my God,*" Louise said. "*But who? Does he live here? How long has it been going on?*

Lindy looked away from her, glancing down at Harry. "Shall we play another?"

"Of course," he said with a nod. "Talking of the old times, are you? Getting reacquainted?"

"Yes," Lindy said.

"Good," Harry said, thrumming the strings of his instrument.

"*We'll talk later,*" Lindy said.

"All right," Louise said, finding herself straining to breathe. And then the words popped out of her mouth. "*I have things to tell you, too.*"

"*You do?*"

"*Oh, yes.*"

"*You've met someone, too?*"

 "*Maybe,*" Louise said.

"*Maybe? Not just maybe. You have met someone, haven't you?*"

Louise felt her mouth contort into an ugly little smile.

"*Yes.*"

"*And what's his name?*"

Louise blushed, blurting out a name.

"*Oh, and what does he do?*"

"*He's a lawyer,*" Louise said.

"*How old is he?*"

"*About . . . forty. He . . . he lives on a ranch outside of Houston.*"

"*Oh, Louise,*" Lindy said, "*I am so happy for you! All this time since Alex . . .*" She reached for Louise, pulling her to her chest. "*Sweetheart. I am so glad to hear. What does he look like? Where'd you meet? Tell me, I want to know everything.*"

Louise drew away from her, trying to catch her breath.

"I'll tell you about it later," she said. *"Would you play a little more music now? I love hearing you and Harry play together."*

"It's sweet, isn't it?" Lindy said. *"And a little bit sad."*

"Shall we?" Louise turned to Harry, who had been waiting during the sisters' private exchange.

She sat apart from them while Lindy and Harry played another song. The moisture in the air, the heat in her body, the years she saw in her sister's face, the time she felt in her own heart—all of it made of the same textures and tones as the melody, and she sat in the midst of it so filled with the hope of the sounds in her ear that she forgot for a brief while the bitterness of her lie.

And then came another tune, and yet another, the sun flowing in like honey through the music room windows, the sweet noise of the plucked strings and the pulsing little shaft of air between her sister's lips and the metal mouthpiece finally convincing her that she might after all know something of what life was about, until the end of the next song when the boy burst into the room to announce that the turtle had eaten one of the carp.

Fast

For as long as we boys could remember, the sun always shone on the Day of Atonement. I would wake up early, listening to the rumbling of my empty stomach, and stare at the brightness of the autumn morning light. My brother, with whom in those years I shared a bedroom at the back of our small house, stayed under the covers while I dressed in my holiday clothes, a heavy broadcloth shirt with a curved collar, thick wool trousers that rasped against my knees and thighs like the steel soap-pads my mother used to scrub the pots, a herringbone tweed sport coat with its label that might have been, for all I knew, an inscription from an Egyptian tomb—*Larkey Bros., Newark*, and on the next line, *Made in the Hebrides*.

"Ollie?" He called to me from his bed, using the nickname that had stuck to me when we went to see an Oliver and Hardy movie when we were both still very young. "You eat yet?"

"I just got up, stupid," I said.

"You going to eat?" he said.

"Not this year," I said.

Since this was a day of fasting, I skipped my usual breakfast of cereal and eggs. Stopping myself in the bathroom when I remembered that I was not even supposed to brush my teeth—because of the water that would pass my lips in the act of brushing—I listened a moment for sounds behind the door of my parents' room and hearing nothing—it was a holiday and so they, hard workers, were sleeping in a bit longer before they too would rise and dress and walk uptown—I descended the stairs and stepped out onto the front porch, breathing the cool salt air that drifted in off Raritan Bay.

Almost at once my friend Rudy came hurrying around the corner, calling to me at distance.

"Y-y-you eat?" He was a short, thin boy whose stutter made him sound younger than he was.

"Nope," I called back as I stepped onto the sidewalk to meet him. "I'm not going to eat this year."

"M-me n-neither." Rudy adjusted his own thick tweed jacket as though it were an infantryman's heavy field-pack.

"We were too young last year," I said, as we started off on our holiday pilgrimage, walking east from my house, on a route that paralleled the river, and then turning north a few streets over.

"W-w-we're old e-e-e-nough," Rudy said. "We c-c-could g-get our n-names in the B-B-Book of D-Death if w-w-we eat this year. The r-r-rabbi said that."

"Who writes it, is what I want to know," I said.

"G-G-God," Rudy said.

"Does he use one of those new ball-point pens?" I said.

"D-d-don't m-ma-make fun," Rudy said.

Our friend Gerald soon came trotting along behind us.

"Hey, you guys, wait up!"

Gerald was dressed as we were in heavy tweeds, except that he had apparently won a concession from his parents on the shirt. While most of its material was pale white like our own, his shirt collar was a shocking shade of pink, the most desirable style of the season.

"J'ou eat?" he said.

Rudy and I shook our heads.

"D-did you?" Rudy said as we walked our northern route toward the center of town.

"Naw," Gerald said. "I ain't had a thing since sundown. We said we were going to fast, right? So the first guy to break it, he's an asshole."

I watched his jaw move up and down as he spoke.

"You chewing gum?" I said. "That counts as eating, you know."

Gerald spat out a wad of gum onto the sidewalk and pointed to his crotch. "Chew this!" he said and hurried along ahead of us.

Like solitary desert travelers who stumble onto a main trade route, we turned west at the next corner and found ourselves in a procession of other early risers, old folks, some families, here and there a few unmarried men, business people or college students, all of them on their way, as we were, to the Orthodox synagogue on the north side of the business district. The town's big movie theater, the Majestic, loomed up on the other side of the street.

```
TODAY ONLY
•7 ACTS VAUDEVILLE 7•
TODAY ONLY
```

The sour smell of beer hovered over the sidewalk as we passed the entrance of the Elks Club and the Blue Moon Grill just next door, dodging the delivery man who rolled a huge steel keg down the loading ramp and bounced it on the cement. He stared at us as we paraded past, and I turned my eyes away, a little ashamed at being dressed for a holiday in the middle of the workaday week. My stomach rumbled again and twisted beneath my belt like a knotted handkerchief and it sounded to me almost as loud as the bounding kegs of beer as they hit the pavement and rolled along.

The traffic light stopped us at the corner of Madison and Smith, the hub of the business district. I stared up at the sky, seeing a few large white clouds sail past with a speed I hadn't ever before noticed. Just ahead lay the antique Eastern synagogue with its golden rounded domes and stained-glass windows. Dozens of people were already gathered on the wide marble steps.

Among them was my older cousin Herb, just back from the war in Korea. With his square jaw and thick brown head of hair and broad smile, he made religion seem as brisk and invigorating as a pickup game of basketball on a late spring afternoon. At his urging—he had been there for an hour already and had just stepped outside for a breath of air, he explained—we climbed the steps and into the foyer with its musty old wood and smoky veil of stale breath and pushed right ahead through another set of doors into the sanctuary itself.

The noise at first was so thick and confusing you couldn't tell if it was sound or light or smell. Sunlight poured down through stained-glass windows high above the women seated in the gallery that girdled the space on three sides while the men below—at our level, that is—rocked back and forth at varying speeds led in ragged song by the white-shawled cantor on the dais as he stood before the open curtains of the elaborately carved cabinet—the Ark—where the holy scrolls were kept.

After hours and hours of sitting and standing in the middle of this roaring ocean of devotional sound, as if spewed out of the contracting belly of a whale, we boys found ourselves back out on the marble steps, hungry, if I can speak for all of us, as we hadn't been since this time last year.

"Oliver?" My father spoke to me on my way down to the sidewalk—he and my mother and brother were climbing up.

"We're getting some fresh air," I said, pointing to my two pals as I walked.

"Oliver," my mother said, just, I think, to say my name.

I didn't look back as the three of us rushed along to the corner, turned east on Smith Street, and stopped by the window of the Fanny Farmer candy store.

"My mouth is watering," Gerald said.

I stared at the beautiful chocolates while reaching up to my head and whisking off my skullcap and stuffing it into my jacket pocket. I was salivating, too.

Just then out of the store came a swarthy boy about our height, his tie askew, his jacket slung over his shoulder.

"You dummies hungry?" Mark Kapelman said. We could see the chocolate smeared around the edges of his lips.

"Y-y-you ate s-something?" Rudy sounded truly surprised.

"No, assface, I went in there for a swim." Mark reached with his free hand into his pocket and came up with a cigar-shaped object wrapped in gold foil. "Want one?"

I shook my head while Gerald took it from his hand.

"I got something else, too," Mark said, digging again into his pocket. He produced some tickets that he held so close to my nose I could almost taste the acrid ink and paper.

We walked to the foot of Smith Street and tossed stones against the wooden gate of the ferry slip. I counted the number of small waves that broke against the rocks on the jetty each minute: eight. We walked a circular route that took us along the water, up High Street, and back to Smith again. Several wasted hours later, we handed our tickets to a skeleton-thin man in a loose-fitting blue jacket beneath the marquee of the Majestic and strolled down the aisle to take our seats.

Eight or nine old men, many of them bald, sat scattered about the large auditorium. Some of them turned to stare at us, and I looked away from their mouths, dark ovals of missing teeth, just as the house lights went down and a small band began to play a tinny but lively tune.

"Hooray for Hollywood," sang a little man in red bow tie and baggy blue suit who stepped from the shadows at the rear of the stage into a growing pool of light at the front. When he finished his song he addressed us.

"Germs . . . I mean, gentlemen . . . no ladies here today, of course . . ." And he continued with a long skein of unfunny lines, preparing us for the afternoon's entertainment. "Seven acts, count 'em, seven," he said, and stepped back into the shadows.

Four women old enough to be our mothers slouched into the light wearing shiny blouses and loose-fitting shorts and began to juggle mallets, then hats, then shoes, then roller skates. Next came a troupe of tired poodles leaping lazily through a set of hoops. The band changed its tune. I got up and went to the bathroom, where from the urinals arose a stale and salty odor like dead horseshoe crabs and seaweed from our local beach. When I returned to my seat the band was playing "Oklahoma" while a gray-haired man stepped into the dark, dragging behind him a large male dummy with enormous red ears, the curtains closing as he disappeared.

"You missed it," Mark Kapelman said, passing me a foil-wrapped chocolate bar. "Here."

"Naw," I said.

"Take it for later," he said. "It ain't going to bite you."

I took the candy bar and stuck it in my pocket, out of my sight.

"Come on out, honey," one of the old men called out into the dark.

"Just a minute, big boy," came a response from the speakers as the curtains parted to reveal a small dollhouse in the middle of the otherwise darkened stage.

"*Come on-a my house,*" a voice warbled over the scratchy sound system as a grass-skirted marionette, ringlets of flowers on her wrists and two large blossoms covering her ample bosoms, swung onto the front of a little balcony. While the band played a shrill and jumpy mambo, the creature swayed and twisted at the behest of some twirling wires, turning and leaping before us, shedding flowers as she moved while old men cried out *More! More!* and I leaned so far forward in my seat that my chin nearly rested on the back of the chair in front of me. Within minutes, I had pulled the foil-wrapped bar from my pocket, ripped open the covering, and jammed the candy into my mouth in the dark.

All our mouths were smeared with chocolate when we emerged, blinking, into the late afternoon light, but we managed with handkerchiefs and spit to clean ourselves up before returning to the synagogue.

"Where have you been?" asked my father who stood with cousin Herb midway up the broad marble steps.

"The Temple," I said, as my friends continued up the steps and disappeared into the building.

"I didn't know you were thinking of joining the Temple," my cousin said, staring at my lips. "What's the matter, too many rules for you here?"

"It was just a visit," I said.

"You didn't eat yet?" My father looked at me.

"No," I lied.

"Your brother couldn't take it," Herb said. "Your mother took him home to make him something to eat."

"Maybe next year," my father said. Taking me by the arm he led me up the steps and into the building. Squeezed onto a bench between him and Herb I spent the next noisy hour trying to decipher the foreign language in the prayer book while the light outside the stained glass windows faded toward night. The day had gone so fast I could hardly catch my breath. Next year, next year for certain, next year, I told myself, next year I would go hungry.

Hernando Alonso

Hernando Alonso was the first Jew to come to Mexico.
He arrived in 1521.

—Vol.XX, *Publicaciones*,
Archivo General de la Nación, Mexico, 1932

*C*iudad de Mexico, Autumn, 1528 — A
bell clangs and he, with the great difficulty of an old man with stiff limbs
and creaking bones, sits up in the dark, awakened from a sleep that had
taken him far away from the high stench of his own urine and ordure in the
far corner of the cell, away from the shouts and cries of madness and pain
in the night.

Hernando Alonso is back.

He had been dreaming a strange and fluent dream, an excursion to far
places to which he had found himself flying like a bird, at one point
soaring over a fleet of brigantines and knowing, even as he looked down,
that it had been their own armada, the very ships that had so long ago carried him and all of the troops of their old commander Cortés from His-
pania to Cuba and then to the shores of this territory that he had called
home for nearly seven years.

There had been battles along the way, and there had been forests, and
the conquerors on horseback had won the battles, with some help from the

local tribes angry with the ruling Aztecs, and, after winning, the soldiers had cut down many trees so that the plain would look more like home and set the pigs to rooting which had the double effect of feeding the troops and destroying more trees. In the rising noise of the prison in early morning Alonso could still hear the barks and screams of those early wars.

In these last few weeks, because of the interrogation by the black-robed Dominican, he had been casting his mind back to those years, and back a lot further as well.

Where were you born?

He had been born in Condado de Niebla in the Year of Our Lord 1460.

Who were your parents?

His dear mother, his dear father, he gave them their names, thinking, as he sometimes did when he was a boy, that some miracle must be going to happen to him because his father had the same name as the father of the Savior. Or perhaps it had already happened. He had come to this new place and lived a long life, free of the terror that had only now fallen upon him in old age.

Siblings?

Two brothers, one older, one younger.

Did you live most of your early life in the town where you were born?

No, the family had moved when he was quite young to Cadiz, a city of water and sails. There he had breathed the sea air in long deep draughts and danced with his brothers along the jetty, dodging the breaking waves in storm. There his father had taught him his trade, carpentry, and then how to work with metal so that he might become a smithy. Hernando Alonso loved to watch the flames leap up from the forge as the odor of burning wood mingled with the sea air in his nostrils. His father initiated him into the secret religion of their forefathers, one of whose rules was that he should eat no pork.

"Stay with me," his mother said to him as she lighted the candles on Friday evenings, casting her eyes about in the small house, as if someone might be watching through the walls. He watched the flames make shadows on the stone wall. He inhaled the smoky odor of the smoldering wicks.

The time in which Hernando Alonso grew into manhood was filled with stories from other cities of funeral pyres piled with burning logs and Jews on fire. On Sundays, at Mass, he shivered in his bones at the stories about devilish Hebrews and the fiery rewards of sin that the priest howled down at them from the altar. Sometimes his mother would take him in her arms on a Sunday evening and hold him, rock him as though he were still a small child.

"Pay no mind," she would say. "For you are a child of Abraham and Isaac. And one day you will pass along to your own children these offices that the Lord has commanded us to perform."

Perhaps it had something to do with the ocean, but the flames kept away from his town.

Ever since Hernando had been a small child he had listened avidly to the stories of the voyages around the coast of Africa made by Portuguese explorers, and then, after he came into his manhood, to news of the Spanish voyages to the New World. His younger brother Gonzalo made a success in the ships-handler trade. Hernando came to visit with his brother at the docks. Now and then he saw Jews like themselves, strangers from other cities, carrying bags full of their belongings in feeble attempts to board ships for North Africa. Once he saw a girl in one of these groups, dark brown eyes, hair braided into two long ropes, and he lingered on the pier nearby, watching her as though he were an animal and she were his prey. The King's guards came along and took the people away in a cart. Hernando watched until he could no longer see the figure of the girl huddled against the side of the cart.

Why should he remember this girl? He couldn't say. It was difficult for him to meet girls his own age from families like his own. No one wanted to let others know how they prayed in secret. It was a paradox, his father explained, though he did not use that word. If they met to practice their religion, they would be found out. And so they stayed solitary, unable to celebrate in the way that their religion decreed. He, the middle son, had not yet married.

It was not a good way to live. But it was the only life they had.

His older brother, Henrique, vowed to find another way. He signed on for a voyage to Africa and when the ship was reported lost, their mother had fallen sick and died shortly thereafter. Then, when Hernando was in his thirties, still unmarried, his father died, leaving him with the shop and the tools. Gonzalo came home one day from the docks shouting about good news from across the water. An expedition mounted by the Crown had returned with word about new land on the other side of the great ocean. In his heart, Hernando felt a deep longing, a tingling that worked through his chest when he thought such things, wanting to sail away from this place of subterfuge and silence with the fearful flames flickering on the horizon.

But in the end, it hadn't been his heart that had taken him across the sea to the new world, it had been his hands. When the call went out along the docks, he was a man in mid-age but nevertheless he signed on as a ship's carpenter on the royal expedition. Gonzalo had known for years the ship's captain who would pilot one of the boats in Cortés's fleet and had made it possible for Hernando to sail west with the would-be conquerors. Gonzalo stood weeping at the dockside and Hernando's own eyes turned wet, but he did not let the tears flow, fearful that the rough sailors who passed along the rail would take it as a sign of weakness. When the land sank down beneath the waters to the east, a large part of his heart sank with it.

The passage was rough, the ships meeting awful, heaving seas. Alonso, along with many others, suffered moments of cold and disabling fear. Even the toughest of the soldiers sometimes worried at the thought of death by water. On the deck during the day the wind-swept water often doused Hernando's working flames. In the dark of night, he lay on his narrow bunk, listening to the moans of the other men, some of them sick, some of them terrified, some, like him, suffering a mixture of physical illness and terrible emotion. The stink below punished him with every intake of breath. His stomach rose and sank, rose and sank, and he pictured his body in a similar motion, bobbing up and down beneath the waves.

I must not give in, he said to himself. In the darkest moment of the voyage, with the noise of the very core of the ship cracking, creaking, whining loud in his ears, he urged himself out of the hold and up the quaking stairs and onto the billowing deck. There he saw the outline of another man against the inky terror of the sky.

"Who goes there?" he said.

"Estrada," the man said, and then heaved his guts over the side of the quavering ship. After a moment, he regained his composure and asked the name of his interrogator.

"It is the ship's carpenter," Alonso said into the mouth of the boiling wind. And then as if God Himself had taken him by the waist with his Holy Thumb and Forefinger, he felt himself doubling over and spitting up all of the contents of his stomach, more than he had ever dreamed he could have held there.

"You are my brother," the soldier said when Alonso had done and the two of them staggered back toward the mast.

"I?"

"Yes, we are Brothers of the Necessary Regurgitation," Estrada said, managing to find a laugh in the middle of this frightful fury of a storm. He crossed himself and made quick recitation of the creed, his serious thanks to the powers that kept them alive in the midst of this maelstrom of whirling wind and surging sea. Then he bid Alonso a good night, warning him not to stay on deck too long.

As soon as the soldier had disappeared below, Hernando Alonso dropped to the salty wet planking and put his hands to his face, saying quietly, "Please, Dear Lord, Lord of Abraham and Isaac, spare me a watery death! Oh, spare me, spare me, I pray You." And then, just to be sure, he reached for the crucifix that he wore about his thick neck and held it cupped in his hands as the thick waves broke over his feet. The wind howled about the tops of the mast, the voice of evil hellhounds chasing after his soul.

"Spare me, Oh, Lord," Hernando Alonso prayed, "and I will dedicate my life to the duties of your Holy Person."

In Cuba, an island of sweet breezes and warm nights filled with the cries of calling birds and the odor of tobacco smoke and charcoal, Hernando Alonso set up as a blacksmith and serviced the horses of Cortés's army while the leader took up his post as governor. The blacksmith knew nothing about politics, though he perked up at the rumor—he heard it from his old shipmate Estrada—that Cortés was planning to sail for Mexico. When the time came, Hernando sailed with him and his army and during the year of war between the Spaniards and the various eastern Mexican tribes, he put to good use his perfected skills as a blacksmith, repairing the steel of weapons, as well as reshoeing the horses so necessary to the victories over the wretched, superstitious Indians.

The expedition's doctor cut open the body of a fallen Mexican and showed off the lungs, much larger organs than those of a flatland Spaniard. On many a night during their march of conquest toward the central plateau, Hernando Alonso lay by the encampment fire and felt his own breath come short, wondering if he would be able to live a comfortable life at this altitude. The crackling of the flames sometimes kept him awake and he listened attentively to the beating of his heart. All of a sudden he felt himself in the center of a great emptiness, a lonely life that was now an uphill climb, weighed down by the clatter of his tools, and so far from the place of his childhood that he felt almost physical pain when he dwelled on it.

First sight of the great Aztec city in the center of the lake—it took his breath away! The marketplace with its astonishing flowers and odors and plumage and painted scrolls! monkeys and rabbits and large striped cats, and many other animals, some with fur, some with scales, for which he had no names! And the tastes! the tastes alone took his mind away and sent him soaring—chocolate and sugar and meat flavored with garlic! Fish from the great lake, and here atop this broad plateau that it had taken them months to reach, fish from the ocean as fresh as if they had just been pulled from the waves!

And of course the people, these Indians as regal and beautiful and handsome and healthy as gods out of stories. None of the other wretched tribes they had met had prepared them for the presence of these Aztecs. The eyes of the women were like still ponds, their irises like floating lilies. The muscles on the arms of the men rippled like water in wind as they paddled the small boats across the lake. Everyone wore gold and jewelry made of exquisite shells and slender braids of rope. You stared at them and they did not look away as did all the other Indians they had encountered.

"These Aztecs believe they are descended from the gods," Estrada said to him at a meal after their first night in the great city.

"If they were not pagans, they would be blasphemers," said Friar Pedro de la Manca, one of the Franciscans who had accompanied them from Cuba. "We are all the children of God, but these Aztecs claim direct descent."

"As if each were Christ Himself?" Estrada said, pulling a piece of meat from a wooden skewer and holding it to his nose. "What is this?" He turned to Hernando Alonso.

"Rabbit?" Hernando Alonso said.

"You are not eating it?" Estrada said.

"Rabbit does not like my stomach," he said.

The Franciscan laughed and reached toward the fire for a skewer of the crackling meat.

"It goes against his religious convictions to eat rabbit," the friar said.

Hernando Alonso glanced at the priest and then looked into the fire. He did not know what to say.

"There are brothers in our order who believe the same," the friar said.

"Then Alonso may join," Estrada said. "He lives already like a monk."

Hernando Alonso turned shyly toward the friar and said, "He means that I have never married."

"Yes, that is a test for our order," the friar said.

"And he knows some who have failed this test," Estrada said with a mouth full of rabbit.

A shadow fell over them and they looked up to see an Aztec child holding a large beautifully shaped jug.

"Yes, my child?" the friar said.

The Indian boy held out the jug.

"They may be gods of some sort," Estrada said, "since they know when a man is thirsty before he even asks."

"They have good manners," said the friar. "Certainly in heaven all souls possess the best of manners."

"Yes," Hernando Alonso said, reaching for the jug.

"Yes?" said Estrada.

"Yes, I am thirsty," Hernando Alonso said. "Sitting by this fire . . ."

"The air up here on this plateau, the intensity of the sun, it does make a man thirsty," said the friar

"And the fires at night," Estrada said. "They make a man sweat even in this cold night air."

Hernando Alonso looked into the leaping flames, took a deep breath, inhaling the marvelous aroma of the roasting meat. He felt that he should say something more about this, but he was not certain as to what. He opened his mouth to speak—probably a foolish thing to do in the company of the friar—when the Indian boy motioned to him. From a sack at his waist, the boy produced a small cup for each man.

"This liquor," Estrada said after a tentative sip. "It is . . ."

"Heavenly," the friar said. "Like ichor. The blood of the pagan gods. Delicious and rejuvenating." He raised a cup to his lips and savored the aroma. He drank. He sighed. "Ichor, yes."

"Blasphemy," said Estrada.

The friar laughed. "We are so far from Spain, so close to heaven up here on this plateau. Who knows what is blasphemy and what is not?"

Hernando Alonso joined in the laughter and the drinking while the rabbit meat sizzled on the skewers.

The flames stretched toward the stars on the night of the great battle, the night the Mexicans came to call the Noche Triste. On that night, Hernando Alonso's talents served the army well. The ship's carpenter oversaw the construction of the thirteen bridges to the city so that the Spanish troops could enter in force. He had crossed the main bridge himself just behind the archers, and later that night walked over the bodies of Aztecs that littered the great square, thinking to himself how much this seemed like a dream of a battle, not a battle itself. The fire! the screaming! the stench of blood and feces! the roar of dying animals fading away as the night faded into early morning and a great star sparkled in the eastern sky.

For his part in the conquest of the Aztec capital, Alonso was awarded land and cattle and some Indian captives to be used as slaves. These he set to work clearing a ranch where he raised imported cattle and, forgive him, Oh, God of Abraham and Isaac, hogs for sale to the army for meat. His brother had come to join him. Only two years after Hernando had sailed for the New World, the Spanish Court issued the Edict of 1523, forbidding Jews, Moors or other heretics from taking up residence in New Spain. So Gonzalo had used his friendship with a sea captain and a forged document in order to gain entry to these new lands under the name of Morales. Hernando Alonso traveled to the port of the True Cross to meet Gonzalo's ship. They talked as they made the trip up through the mountains and talked more when they reached the plateau.

"This is a good piece of land they have given you," Morales said.

"I am grateful for it," said Alonso.

"And do they know you are a Jew?"

"I am what I am. I have never hidden anything. I believe what I believe and I have gone to Mass in the church that we have built on the place where the Aztec temple stood."

"It is a crime," Morales said, "for a Jew to cross the border into New Spain. We are both criminals in the eyes of the Crown."

Alonso said, "I have helped the Crown win mighty victories."

"You raise swine for the soldiers of the Crown. And in turn they would call you a hog."

"No one calls me anything but my own name. Hernando Alonso. That is what they call me. That is who I am. Hernando Alonso."

After the victory Mass that had been celebrated in the church where the pagan temple had stood, attendance by the old soldiers dwindled. Alonso became enamored of one of his female slaves and freed her and married her in this same church. This girl had the large brown eyes typical of the Aztecs and her voice in her language sounded to his ears like music.

"Look at your hair. It is turning white," his brother said. "Are you certain you are ready for this new life?"

Hernando Alonso nodded.

"My life has always surprised me. And so if love has come to me—"

"Love?" His brother shook his head in amazement.

"That is what it is," Hernando Alonso said. "Love has come to me late in life, and I have always been waiting for it though I never thought that it would take this long to arrive. Now that it is here, I embrace it."

From another room of the new stone farmhouse, his new wife's singing floated in like the noise of birdsong over water.

"Have you told her?" his brother said.

"I will tell her," Alonso said. "If we have children, I will tell her."

The priest came to the house to meet with the Indian woman, giving her instruction in the faith.

"She is an intelligent girl," he said. "She learns Spanish quickly and she was quick as well to learn the essentials of the Faith. She should make you a good wife, Hernando Alonso. And a good family."

"I am pleased to hear this," Hernando Alonso said. "I have wanted a family all my life. It has only been an accident that I never married."

"Now you can understand that God has made this plan for you. He wanted you to wait until you had traveled all this distance from your home before you would make a new family. And I know that if you continue to trust in our Lord, Jesus Christ, you will live out long years here in New Spain."

"I trust in Him," Hernando Alonso said.

"Then you have nothing to fear," the priest said.

Hernando Alonso nodded his head in assent, but wondered to himself if the priest suspected that he should be fearful when he was not. But he did not entertain this thought for very long. Even when the priest returned and asked him the same question Hernando Alonso did not worry himself with the thought for more than a moment.

With work and now his family, there was too much else to think about. His wife became pregnant and their first child was baptized in the church that the commander had ordered be constructed on the ruins of the old Aztec temple. It was during this ceremony that old memories flickered like darting flame through his mind. When he returned home after the ceremony Hernando Alonso, much to the dismay of his wife, who feared that one of the servants would see him taking over the function of a priest, dipped his fingers in wine, splashed it on his child's brow, and then drank the rest of the wine in the cup. Staring down at the child's naked body, he thanked the old Hebrew God that a daughter had come to him instead of a son, because he did not have to worry about the problem of circumcision. If the child had been a boy, would he have made the cut himself? No, no, he would have asked his brother. But would *he* have done it?

Nights on the ranch on the high plateau, the sound of the animals lowing in the corrals, skies filled with burning stars that loomed so close it seemed as though you could almost feel the bite of the sparks—he thought himself so fortunate that he had removed himself from the turmoil back home and made this new life for himself. Once the army had defeated the Indians here, a great calm had settled over the center of the territory. He himself had given the rest of his servants their freedom and most of them had stayed on to work at the ranch, many of them taking instruction from the priest when he made his regular visits.

"You trusted in Our Lord Jesus Christ and he has made a good life for you," the priest said. "By your example, you show these pagans how a man should live."

"We have turned their world upside down," Hernando Alonso said. "I hope that they learn how to live a good life in this new world."

"We show them by our examples," the priest said.

"This I hope is true," Hernando Alonso said. But when he and his wife strolled in the center of the city he often noticed the conquerers, turning fat and gray some half dozen years after the end of the war, shouting at Indians, kicking at them, in one instance punching one to the ground for not getting out of the way quickly enough. He loved his wife, and it disturbed him to see her fellow Indians, her family, treated in such a manner. He considered requesting an audience with Cortés and speaking about this, but why would the governor want to hear him, a former ship's carpenter, now a rancher, speak about anything?

There was nothing he could do except conduct himself in the best way he knew how toward his own household and, remembering his shipboard pledge to his God, this is what he proposed to do. In the quiet of their bed he would tell his wife stories from the Five Books of Moses, stories he had learned as a child and which now came back to him in his maturity, and gradually she understood that though they both attended Mass, he still valued the old wisdom of the Jews. Although the news from Spain had it that the Inquisition's fires were burning brightly, fed by the bodies of unrepentant Jews, here on the high plateau of Mexico Alonso felt so distant from such matters that he scarcely gave them a thought. New Spain was a place where he could grow old in peace. The Franciscans avidly attended to the business of converting the Indians. They didn't seem to have time to worry much about the faith of the old soldiers and their retinues.

When the second child came, Hernando Alonso again dipped his fingers in wine and dripped some of the liquid onto the girl's forehead—oh, yes, thank the Lord, another girl!—saying some old but newly recollected words in the Ladino tongue. Other memories jittered flamelike in his mind. As if a thick old wooden door had suddenly swung open, he looked down a long aisle into the almost forgotten past. And he stared long and hard.

One Sunday just before Mass, with his wife in her monthlies, he told her to stay at home.

"Señora," he is reported to have said, "in your present condition thou wouldst profane the Church."

His wife replied, "These are old ceremonies of the Jews which are not observed now that we have adopted the evangelical grace . . ."

When the priest inquired about her, leaning down to pat one of the children on the head, Alonso said, "She is ill." It became his custom, asking her to stay away from Mass when she was in that condition. Whether or not the priest noticed, he never said anything more about it.

Another few years went by, all those ink-black nights beneath the hot and burning stars. The children grew; he and his brother increased their cattle and swine herds tenfold. Hernando Alonso had competition in the bidding but the city council recognized his seniority by accepting his bids over some lower proposals. It didn't hurt that the acting governor of New Spain was his old shipmate Estrada.

Did his rivals speak badly of him? Did they make clear that they knew he was a secret Jew and thus undeserving of special privilege? It didn't matter to him. He was getting to be an old man and believed that he deserved such deference. He remembered the Noche Triste and how it might have been if he hadn't built those bridges to the center of the city. Now and then he would see his old commander at Mass. The graying Cortés looked over at him in knowing fashion, as if to ask, Why does a Hebrew man like yourself suffer this inscrutable pageantry? Corpulent old soldiers kept up their brawling in the taverns and the streets, sometimes even right up to the steps of the churches. The priests spoke to Cortés but he pleaded for his men. Would the Church Itself be here in Mexico without these soldiers?

And then came the spring of 1528. Cactus flowers of all shades of pastels bloomed with an intensity Alonso had never before noticed. Lilies covered the lakes with a creamy efflorescence that reminded him of the foamy milk that had sometimes dripped from the breasts of his wife after one of their daughters had pulled away from the nipple. Perfume of plant and water and smoke swelled the air, and the sky above, a delicate white the same shade as the water-flowers, seemed to settle upon them during the high noon hour like a filmy cloak of heat. The difference between day and night was the difference between one territory and another, one warm, one cool, one bright, one intensely dark. Perhaps it was just the changing of the seasons, perhaps it was that the children were growing older and seemed to him less like sweet young animals and more like cantankerous human beings, but Hernando Alonso noticed within his chest a deep and growing sadness.

His wife sang to him poems in her old pagan tongue, verses she was supposed to have given up and forgotten after her instruction in the True Faith.

> *The gods are like eternal flowers,*
> *and time will kill all but them . . .*

"Sing another," Hernando Alonso said to her when she had finished, knowing that he should not encourage her. But her voice was lovely and soothing, and it took his mind away from the sadness in his chest.

> *Dreams come to us like rain in winter,*
> *In times of drought we die of sleep . . .*

"You make such beautiful music out of the matter of death and killing," he said. She shook her head, gave a little shrug—he found it amazing that such a gesture would be the same among her people and his own. The older he got, the less he knew what he was, the less he understood. These small things he held on to: simple meals with his wife; telling stories to the children; gazing at the burning night sky; walking with his wife and children in the city, pointing out to them where he had been on certain days and nights in the first week or two of the conquest (although omitting, of course, some of the bloodier details).

It was on one such walk, of a quiet afternoon after Mass, that, as they were strolling through the main square, a commotion rose up on the other side of the great space and he guided the family closer so that he might have a look. Whenever such a thing occurred it was always aging conquistadores committing some contrary act, drinking or fighting or both. But on a Sunday? As they walked closer, he watched the dust swirl up around the crowd, as if people were scuffling, or struggling to gain a closer look. He caught only a glimpse of a black robe and a hood before the children tugged at his hands and led him off in the direction of the fountain.

The next day he heard the news, that the Dominican Friar San Vicente de María, sent to Mexico to act in all matters of the Faith and to establish the first monasteries, had arrived in the city. A number of old soldiers were immediately hauled in before a church tribunal to answer for blasphemies and other insults. Still, Hernando Alonso did not worry about himself because his old commander would look after him. Then in May Cortés departed for Spain to plead some grievances before the Crown. Estrada traveled with him. Hernando Alonso was left without a protector.

It didn't take long before San Vicente's men came for him in the night, leaving behind his sobbing wife and sleeping children. The Franciscan friar stood to one side while the Dominican conducted the proceedings. The charges against him were composed of three counts: One, that his children were baptized twice, once by the Franciscan and then again "according to the ritual of the law of Moses." Two, that he refused to permit his wife to attend Mass when she was having her menstrual period. He glanced over at the Franciscan, who dropped his gaze. The third charge? A witness, one of his own former slaves whom he had freed, stated that Alonso poured water over the head of one of the daughters and then drank the water in mockery of baptism. The witness stated also that Alonso sang a psalm that referred to Israel's Lord God of Egypt, "o una cosa de esta manera . . ." (Had he sung a psalm? He could not remember. He remembered many things but he could not remember this.)

Thus Hernando Alonso was found guilty of "Judaizing," the punishment for which was death by fire. He was taken to a dark cell where days went by quickly, like water spilled from a cup. One morning after returning from a long period of questioning by the Dominican, Hernando Alonso found his brother sitting on the floor of his cell.

"The fires that burned in Spain," Gonzalo said. "They have almost caught up with us."

"But why?" Hernando Alonso asked. "I have made a good life here and I have done good things for the territory."

"It is a matter of blood," his brother said.

"Do they want blood? I'll give them some of my blood in exchange for life. I'll give them a cup of it. A glass. A bottle full of it."

"Our blood is no good to them," his brother said. "They say it is different from theirs. It sullies their veins. They want to purify the bloodlines of New Spain just as they have in the old country."

"Why is our blood impure?" Hernando Alonso said.

His brother held out empty palms before him.

He asked himself the question when his wife was allowed to visit him, staring at her skin that was the color of beautifully worked leather, at the brown pools of her eyes. What kind of blood ran in her veins? He had never thought about her blood. He had never thought to look at her in this manner; he had never looked at her in any other way but admiration for her beauty.

"Are you cold at night?" she said.

He shook his head. "My anger keeps me warm," he said.

"I went to see the priest."

"And what did he say?"

"He did not know what he could do."

"He did not know?"

"That is what he told me."

Hernando Alonso, as old as he was, began to cry like a child. "All my years, it comes to nothing. The work I made for them. And the children, what will become of them?"

"The priest told me that he would help with the children," his wife said.

He tried to stop his tears. After a while he stopped them. "I believe that he will keep his promise."

"He said that he is very sorry," his wife said.

"I believe that as well," Hernando Alonso said.

The priest said this himself a few days later when he came to the cell.

"Thank you," Hernando Alonso said.

"I wish I could do more," the priest said.

"You can answer a question," Hernando Alonso said.

"What is your question?"

Hernando Alonso asked him about the matter of blood, and the priest could not give him a reply.

"But what can you do to help me?" he asked the priest.

The priest did not speak. But even in the dim light of the dungeon Hernando Alonso saw an answer in his hooded eyes.

"Leave me now," he said. "I am tired and I want to sleep. The worry about dying has made me very tired. You would think I would want to stay awake for every moment allowed to me. But my body feels weighed down by stones the size of a pyramid."

"I understand," the priest said. He cleared his throat as if to say more.

"Please, go," Hernando Alonso said.

The priest made a noise like a blessing and departed into the shadows of the jail.

Hernando Alonso went to sleep and dreamed that same dream of flying above the rows of ships in the midst of a pale-green, pacific ocean, and he wished his initial passage had been that calm.

Later that same evening Estrada appeared at his cell door. "My friend," he said.

"Your soon-to-be late departed friend," Hernando Alonso said.

"I understand why you are bitter. Perhaps there is no other way to be."

"I do not understand anything. All the years that I have lived on earth and I do not understand a single thing."

"Please understand one thing. That I am thinking of your situation. And that I am working for you."

"What do you mean?"

"There is a way."

"A way out?"

"Yes."

"Tell me."

Estrada leaned closer to the door. "One of the guards is the son of a man who once worked for me. I will speak to his father tonight."

"But not to him directly?"

"I believe it is best to speak to his father first."

"If you say so. But, please, do it tonight. They have promised to come for me tomorrow morning."

"I know, my friend. But I only just discovered this news. I will do it. And we will come for you before the sun rises."

"And where will I go?"

"To the north," Estrada said. "There is plenty of territory there to hide in."

"To the north? A long way? I'm . . . very tired. My bones have grown so cold while lying here."

"You will have a horse. Or a burro. You will not have to walk."

"And my wife and children?"

"Perhaps we can arrange for them to follow later."

"Can't they come with me tomorrow?"

Estrada shook his head. "It is too dangerous. One man, we can arrange for. But a family?"

"Good. Then I will see them later."

"Yes, of course. You will see them later. And you will see me sooner."

"Thank you, my friend," Hernando Alonso said, pushing his hand between the bars in order to touch his friend's hand.

He tried to sleep. But it was foolish to try. He would have plenty of time to sleep after he made his way north. Until Estrada's man appeared to free him—what was the rest of the plan? he didn't know—he would remain alert, ready to flee at a moment's notice. Even as darkness settled over the prison and the others in the cells nearby—murderers, thieves, vandals, most of them—sank into a temporary oblivion that passed for peace, he became more and more attentive to the sounds and the movements around him. Somewhere in the dark, a man was coughing. Another sounded as though he were saying prayers, but his voice was too indistinct to tell for certain.

And what prayers do I know? Hernando Alonso asked himself. Not many. Only one, perhaps.

Hear, O Israel, the Lord is God, the Lord is One.

Yes, he remembered this phrase dimly out of his childhood, the way he remembered the sight of a tall ship with sails full blown passing out of the harbor. See, his father said, they are off for an adventure.

Hear, O Israel, the Lord is God, the Lord is One.

Whatever that meant.

He pictured his father standing tall beside him, he could almost feel the pressure of the man's rough hand around his own small hand. He could smell the harbor, the mix of salt sea and moss and dying fish and the ropes and the tar, the sweetness of the wooden planks, the smoke from cooking fires along the piers.

Why is it that, when you near the end of life, you think more and more about the beginnings?

Well, in the north country, perhaps he might have the time to ponder these questions before his wife and children arrived.

A COCK CROWED in the darkness. And crowed again.

He must have slept.

Yes, because he remembered a dream. Of ships on the high seas, and stars revolving rapidly overhead, and giant fish with swords for beaks leaping out of the water and passing him by, so close that he could look directly into their wide gaping eyes, and he stood upon a deck, and the deck heaved as the seas broke across it, and there came the sounds of war, of cannons exploding mixed with the crash of the seas on the thick wooden planking, and he trembled, because he did not want to die.

The cock crowed a third time, and the jailor appeared.

"Thank God," Hernando Alonso said. "You are the friend of Estrada?"

"Who?" the man said. His breath smelled sourly of undigested corn.

"You are here to help me, yes?"

The jailor, a short man with rough hands, fumbled with the keys. "I am here to help you pass into the next world."

"Please, don't joke," Hernando Alonso said. "I am ready to go. Open the door."

The jailor opened the lock and looked at him, sneered, almost. "I never met a man in such a hurry. Do you know something about the next world that I don't know?"

"We're going north, aren't we?" Hernando Alonso said.

"North, south, east, west. Directions don't matter on this sort of journey."

"What are you talking about?"

The jailor came toward him, holding out those rough hands. The odor of his breath washed over Hernando Alonso's sweating face.

"Make yourself brave," the jailor said. "They are coming for you."

Hernando Alonso felt terribly old.

Light, suddenly—the day had come. The Dominican priest appeared with the ritual garment that he quickly draped over Hernando Alonso's head and shoulders.

Alonso took short steps as they moved along the route to the plaza, two guards at his side. Surely they were not going to execute him just for being who he was? He, who had crossed the ocean sea to help defeat the pagan Aztec? I am just a man, he said. Only a man. And my children, my children, what of them, what of them? Such questions haunted him as he passed among the rows of people who had come in the early morning light to see him on his way. He smelled cooking fires as if out of his dream. Dawn beamed up behind the great cathedral, making it seem a mere paper cutout lined against the sky.

"Is this a Jew?" he heard someone say.

"It is Hernando Alonso, the rancher," another said.

"And is he a Jew?" A third voice.

"He looks just like a man," another said.

"Yes," Hernando Alonso said—at least he thought that he spoke out loud—"I am just a man, just a man."

He looked for his wife, for his children. Had they come? Had he already passed them by? Tugging aside the garment covering his skull and shoulders, he poked out his head like a turtle peering from its shell, searching the crowd for Estrada. Where was he? Where had he gone? Finally, he thought he saw him, standing off to one side, his friend with his head bowed, as though it were too heavy to lift.

They led Hernando Alonso to a large construction of logs and sticks in the center of the plaza where the Dominican stood waiting for him. This priest said some words, but Hernando Alonso wasn't listening. He was like a man suffering from a high fever who hears only the pounding beat of the pulse within the inflammation of his blood.

Hear, O, Israel, the Lord is God, the Lord is One. I am just a man, I am just a man.

As men in hoods and robes worked with torches around the base of the pyre, he said to himself: Where are the children? the flowers? the lights? father? mother? brothers? my wife? the stars? the fire, the stones, the building, the ocean, the blood? my cows? my pigs? my houses? my children? I am just a man. Smoke rose thickly at his ankles, flames tickled his feet. Was it like this for Jesus when they came for Him? Could He have said such things to Himself as they took Him?

These thoughts tumbled through his mind until he smelled his own flesh burning.

On the Millstone River:
A Story from Memory

These fragments I have shored against my ruins . . .
—T.S.Eliot, "The Wasteland"

Water is best.
—Pindar

1. NOVEMBER, 1963

The news struck me as though it were the very shot itself. I'd been lying on
my bed, in a stupor not unlike the state that years later I would come to
know as "the work trance," the inward-turning thoughtless mood when
words might come, and form images in the otherwise useless mind. The
woman I had been seeing had gone back to school in New Jersey, leaving
me behind to do what it was I did in those days, which was not very much
at all.

The small sterile New York apartment faced on a brick wall in Little
Italy. From the bed where I lay when the telephone rang I could see the
red-tint of the brick, my eyes could follow along the lines, as prisoners
might in cells to which they had been remanded for months or years.
When I wasn't watching the brick I followed the little wisps of dust and hair
that floated across the linoleum-covered floor, shifting here and there on

the flush of drafts so slight I could not feel even the slightest hint of them where I lay on the bed.

At the end of the summer I had returned on a steamship from a year in Europe and had spent hours at the railing, watching the undulating ocean surging up and away in place, waves piling upon waves in such hypnotic fashion that I understood immediately how it was that the sirens called even to the smartest sailors—those who knew in their minds the reality that their eyes betrayed—and drew them over the rail into the sea. The water, the waves, the endless range of whitecaps—the dust-kittens on my linoleum floor sent me dreaming back to those days and nights at sea.

And before that, to the autumn and part of a winter in Europe, where I lived mostly in a small rented apartment with its rear window looking out on the beach in a Spanish fishing village south of Málaga. Friends of mine from college days—not so long ago then—had emigrated there, and there after some weeks in Holland and France I traveled, drawn by an invitation and my great (scarcely conscious) need for companionship, friendship, family.

The train ride from Paris lasted several days, and I read and ate thick slices of bread and good cheese and drank wine from bottles I bought at the station stops along the way. Sometimes my compartment filled with plump bourgeois families, and, as we rolled closer and closer to the Spanish border, with dusky-skinned working men who passed around their bottles as though wine were community property of all the citizens of the world. Their wine tasted stronger and darker than mine. Their cheese tasted of the fields and the barn. The texture and flavor of their bread made you think you were biting into the crust of the earth itself.

Crossing into Spain I stalked heroically in my mind the grim-faced members of the Guardia Civil, Franco's national police, but otherwise passed quietly along, holding out my passport for inspection, carrying my bags to the Spanish train. Another long day, a long night in Madrid, another train, and then darkness, and the car, nearly empty now, rolled to the end of the line, in the Andalusian station at Fuengirola where my square-shouldered friend Jim stood watching for my face in the train window.

"Hey," he said in that South Jersey accent of his, flat but almost drawling at the same time, "how you doing?" He squinted at me, his usual way of looking at things, smiling in the dim light of the low-intensity lamps of the Spanish station.

"Great," I said, thinking I knew the truth of my life.

"Great," he said, believing me, I suppose.

Under cover of night and fog we climbed into his little Spanish car and drove a short distance to his house. After long voyage, I had arrived.

Within a day or so he had introduced me to his landlord, Don Clemente León, a gravelly-voiced entrepreneur who owned a place for me to rent a few streets away right on the beach.

"You must to come to Málaga be my guest," Don Clemente said the morning I moved my few possessions—a couple of bags and a small portable typewriter my parents had given me for graduation—into the apartment at the beach. A day later, a warm autumn day, he appeared at my door with a big smile on his dark unshaven face.

"Come with me, my friend, I want to take you to a marvelous place."

In the old section of Málaga, down narrow streets where balconies leaned out over the passageways and the sky was a brilliant stripe of royal blue stretching between the upper edges of the confining buildings, music played—the deep downward bending agonies of flamenco—and women cried from window to window, children shrieked and laughed, and in the distance you could hear the buzzing and rumbling of motorbikes and buses. The air reeked of cooking oil and diesel and spices as yet unknown to me.

Don Clemente led me along these narrow lanes to an ornate doorway and a steep set of steps which in turn took us to the second story, and a many-roomed apartment with wide windows covered with orange and red brocade. Rose-colored organdy covered the walls. The flavors of incense and flowery perfume filled the corridors. Even as my guide introduced me to a short stump of a woman in a blue dressing gown, I felt as though I had wandered into a giant gift package, the kind of wrapped box you see in the windows of department stores at Christmas. I knew no Spanish, and a brief conversation took place concerning me that I could not understand. Within moments the woman reached for my hand and led me into one of the bedrooms. Out of the corner of my eye I watched Don Clemente talking with another woman who was dressed in the same fashion as my companion.

Then he was gone.

"*Listo?*" she said, motioning toward me.

I understood nothing except the gesture. She undid her robe and lay back on the narrow bed as though I were a physician and had arrived to examine her.

Shouts and curses came from somewhere nearby in the house.

I untied my shoes and stepped out of them and was fumbling with my trousers when a sudden chill overcame me as certainly as if I were a wader through some northern stream.

"*Andale, andale,*" the woman said, pulling open her robe to reveal her chest, thick with heavy flesh of rubbery dugs, her scarred, rippled belly and dark bramble beneath. My legs began to tremble—from the chill, I told myself, from the chill. But at her insistence I let my trousers fall and stepped out of them and moved closer to the bed. Seeing that she had closed her eyes, I reached down and slid my wallet from my trouser pocket and slipped it into my coat pocket.

"*Amor,*" she said, blinking open her eyes to stare up at me.

"Yes," I said, "yes," and trouserless but still wearing my sport jacket and my shirt climbed up on the bed and hovered over her, shivering from fear, from lust, while she adjusted herself to take my weight. And then I remembered a story about Flaubert that one of our crowd at school who had read a biography of him—maybe it was my friend Jim himself—retold now and then, about how the great French master had gone to a brothel and mounted a prostitute while still wearing his hat and with a lighted cigarette between his lips.

And I began to laugh at the absurdity of it, and at my own absurdity, and the woman beneath me began to laugh and before I knew it, it was over and I felt nothing except disappointment, and a tinge of worry about the possibility of disease.

Would Flaubert have worried?

BACK IN MY village each morning I settled in, typing for an hour or two—today I can't call it "work" though I might have called it that then—on the Remington portable, later spending some time writing in a small red-bound notebook, jotting down in my loose hand notations about the Andalusian light and the air and the sea.

Sometimes at lunch I walked a few dusty streets over, avoiding the piles of mule dung in the road, visiting my friends. Jim had been a year ahead of me at school, and of all our crowd seemed to us destined to become one of the best writers of our generation. Only a few stories and some elusive scraps of manuscript proved that to us—to me, anyway—but the talk that arose from this small amount of work was voluminous, like nothing I'd heard before. We saw ourselves as the offspring of the Beats—Burroughs, Ginsberg, Kerouac our gods—who were trying to find our way back to older deities, to Melville and Hawthorne, to Joyce, and Flaubert and Stendhal, to Dostoyevsky. We read, we talked, we ranted, and wrote little that I remember.

Of all our crowd, Jim alone was singled out by love. He was married to Renate, a gentle, olive-skinned nurse whom he had known since high school in Camden, New Jersey. She was voluptuous and sweet-voiced, with a manner so easeful that at the approach of this healer all illness faded in you before it began. If love could engender good writing, then Jim should have been a great one from the start. No one in our crowd was as much loved as Jim. After graduation, while I was working as a toll collector on the New Jersey Turnpike, I saved my money for passage to Europe so that I could live near Jim and Renate.

On days when I stayed in the apartment and "worked" through lunch I might take a break and eat some fruit on the rear patio, watching the waves flowing in from North Africa splash on the Spanish sand. Sometimes Jim joined me for a walk along the waterline, and we talked about our grand visions. I had just read *This Side of Paradise* on the train and found it something less than a triumph.

"Try to do a book like that yourself," Jim said.

"I will," I said, staring into the wind. A long line of haze obscured the distant African shore.

"You and that donkey," Jim said, pointing to the tethered beast that stood with its neck bowed toward the loose pile of straw its caretaker had tossed onto the sand before it.

"You'll see," I said to Jim.

"Holy shit," he said, and I thought for a moment that he was responding to my bold and ignorant declaration. Then I followed his eyes up to where he was staring, at a large cloud that had drifted up over the Mediterranean.

"Do you see it?" he said.

"Yeah," I said.

"Shaped just like a cross," he said.

"You're right," I said.

"Some kind of sign," Jim said.

"Of what?" I said.

"How the hell do I know?" Jim said. "But I'll bet it has something to do with something. It's all connected, you know. I'm not sure how, but sooner or later we're going to find out."

"When?" I said. "I want to know now."

"No, you don't," Jim said. "You think you want to know, but you don't really."

"I do," I said.

"No, you don't," he said.

"I do," I said. "That's why I'm here. That's why I came all this way."

"You came to Fuengirola to find something out?"

"To Europe," I said. "To Spain."

Jim turned away to spit into the sand.

"Let me know when you got it figured," he said and started walking up the beach. I tagged along after him. He was slightly older than I was, he was married, he had been here longer on these old shores. Surely he knew things he could impart to me about life, about literature. But when I caught up with him he just gave a shrug and laughed and threw an arm over my shoulder and led me back to his house for a meal.

After dinner, I walked along the dusty street that led to my new lodgings, climbed the steps, listening to the racket of the donkey braying at the waves. From the rear window of the apartment the ocean seemed almost invisible in the darkness. I could hear it, but I couldn't see it. From the front window I spied a fleshy girl dressed in a short skirt silhouetted in the doorway of the small stone house directly across the shadowy street. She was, I soon learned, the daughter of a local fisherman. She seemed to be staring up to where I stood as though she knew I was watching her.

I HAD NOT yet turned on a light inside the apartment, but she smiled up at my window. I looked away. Now and then she sashayed out into the street, swinging her hips with the force of Atlantic tides, hoping, I surmised, to lure me into an encounter on the rough pavement. Opening her eyes wide, she stared, and then lowered her eyes, in a rhythm as old as any music.

We met only once on the street, by accident (on my part, at least).

"*A dónde vas?*" she said.

I didn't understand.

"*A dónde vas?*" she asked me again, her voice tinged with a certain annoyance and frustration.

But I hadn't yet learned any Spanish. And if I had understood, what could I have said? I didn't know where I was going.

A LITTLE MORE than half a year later, the sea, carpeted by whitecaps, engaged me for almost a week on the way home, the same waters that splashed in gentle breakers on the beach outside my apartment window, those waters having flowed past the Straits of Gibraltar, into the Atlantic, buoying up my steamship. Whenever the light allowed I went to the rail to admire the heaving, posturing performance of the open ocean, feeling the pulse of the oldest attraction toward nothingness beating upon my chest. In morning light, with a good wind whipping across the wave-tops, the sea appeared to be frozen all the way to the horizon where the sharp outline of the tallest waves seemed to stand still against a pale blue sky. I stared and gazed, gazed and stared. Come and walk, a voice came to me. Come and take a step or two, see if it will hold you. But I held tightly to the rail, feeling the wind trying to lift my body as though it were a sail or a kite. I stared at the water, I stared at it hard and long as if at any moment some answer to all the questions I was still too mute to ask might come bobbing up from beneath the waves. Where was I going? Where had I been?

I stood at the rail most of the afternoon, feeling—I couldn't have said then what it was I was feeling, but this may be it—feeling the water in my body speaking to the water surrounding us. At sunset the light stretched over the sea like opalescent canvas, as if to wrap the very liquid of the planet in a package that might be delivered intact to some other location in the universe. And when it became too dark to study the waves, I wandered through the ship, hoping some luck might strike me and bring me something I desired, if only I knew what that was. In the top bunk of the two-decker bed in my little cabin, the other fellow who shared the room having gone off to the bar, I grappled with the bra-hooks belonging to a slender Chinese-American girl from Chicago who that afternoon had stepped up beside me at the rail while I was counting waves. She unloosed my trousers and sucked me into her mouth as though she were slurping an ice cream soda. I writhed on the bed, as much from the novelty of it as the pleasure. When she pulled away from me, strands of liquid dripped from her lips as though she were an animal and had just drunk from a desert waterhole. I don't know that I have ever been so happy to break away from something so pleasurable as when we finished our labors and she jumped lightly down onto the cabin floor, leaving me behind on the upper bunk to feel the oceanic rocking I had forgotten in the frenzy of our coupling.

One of the last nights of our passage I went up on deck quite late to find some drunken passengers tossing deck chairs over the rail at the stern. I recognized one of them as the Chinese girl from Chicago and did not step forward to join her. After a moment I retreated below deck, to emerge only after breakfast the next morning when I stood at the rail again, trying to figure out my place in the scheme of things: this vast expanse of churning salt water, the saliva I felt sloshing about in my mouth, the sperm I had spurted past that Chicago girl's lips. It was all connected, as time was, generation after generation marching back in ranks; as air was, all the air circling the planet; as water was, all these seas and oceans linked, all the ponds and lakes connected to them by the process of condensation and storming rain. Of all this, and nothing, I was sure.

When I returned to New York I felt decidedly disconnected. My birth-place lay across the river in New Jersey, a time-warp away. I saw little of my parents, having found the cheap room in Little Italy and a job at a trade newspaper that had offices just north of Greenwich Village. The work consisted mainly of writing daily stories about the prices of animal skins, mostly mink, at the Hudson's Bay Fur Trading Company in mid-Manhattan, and writing weekly stories about auctions elsewhere in the world. Once I got the hang of it, the work was not difficult. Lunchtime expanded to include two-hour chess games at Village cafes; the occasional stick of marijuana became the daily indulgence after chess. At four, I would return to my typewriter at the newspaper office, my head usually swelled with matters

I could not put into words, my notebook filled with numbers from the auction earlier in the day.

At night, I went to movies, plays, parties. The movies were classics — Eisenstein and Dreyer and Griffith and all the other greats. It was an education in film I gave myself for which I had no equivalent in letters. The theater was mostly experimental. No musicals. Nothing much actually on Broadway. Instinct sometimes sent me to the right places. On a rooftop stage on Houston Street Zero Mostel played Leopold Bloom and Siobhan McKenna his Molly Bloom.

New York in those days for someone in his twenties was a stewpot, a hotbed, a brothel and a convent, a drawing room and a bedroom, a tearoom and a kitchen, a closet and a veranda, streets and avenues and alleys and dead ends, walk-ups and skyscrapers, all of them filled with women. I met women in the park, I met women on the street, young women, older women, women fresh out of college, women who had worked for years as sales clerks in Village shops, women who thought nothing of giving themselves to me for a night in exchange for a place to sleep, women for whom a few words of kindness were everything, women for whom cruelty was kindness, women of few words, women whose tongues wagged like the tails of friendly dogs, women who liked themselves, women who hated themselves, women who loved their parents, women who despised them, married women, divorced women, virgins, whores, devout women, atheist women, capitalist women, communist women, dark women and pale women, Jewish women and Gentile women, ugly and pretty, women with mouths as fresh as roses, women whose breath reeked of all the bars they'd ever frequented.

Yet all these encounters seemed somehow peripheral to my yearning. A year had gone by since I had left the country, and I had crossed the ocean twice in order to leave and return. Something had changed in me that I could not name, and something seemed to have changed in the world. It was growing a little darker and colder, the wind growing more sharp. Turn a corner and you might feel the cool draft blowing in off one of the rivers.

Look uptown toward infinity and the wind would flow back over you after a journey all the way from the pole to the north.

Indian summer arrived, and the air warmed up, giving the impression that the season just ended might have come again. Though I sweated in the unseasonable heat, I understood that summer was over. Something else was going on in my life and I grappled with the feeling, trying desperately to understand it.

Nothing helped. I went to movie after movie, sometimes two, even once in a while three movies a day. I could lose myself in the dark cool theaters, in the bright dramas flashing on the screen. But when the lights came up, I was left with myself again, vaguely uncomfortable, not so much unhappy or bored as feeling only incidentally connected to the life going on around me.

A young woman with sturdy legs, wild dark eyes and bad teeth followed me off a bus and caught up with me in front of the New York Public Library. We stood on the library steps and talked and it quickly became clear to me that she had something she wanted desperately to give me. I called her the next day. For weeks I paid her visits at night at her apartment about a ten-minute walk from my own, dutifully performing the part she had written for me in the scenario of her own desire. In this odd affair I enjoyed the way I felt after I left her bed, not while I was in it.

Another woman sometimes came to my apartment, playing the same role for me as I played for the girl I had met on the bus ride. And there was a pretty dark-haired Jewish woman who wore only the finest skirts and blouses and flirted with me at work. Now and then we met on the fire stairs, hugging, kissing, nothing more. She was married to a travel agent with an office nearby and would not allow me to accompany her to lunch. I met another girl at work, the daughter, as it happened, of a woman who had known my mother in high school. She was flighty, with dark wiry hair and cheerful blue eyes, and we spent a few weekends together in her apartment. She had a pubic patch as coarse as a Brillo pad and we rubbed a rash above my pubic bone that nearly bled each time we connected.

Chasing, kissing, entering these women, it was all like a dream, or a dream of a dream. None of them seemed as real to me as the actresses I saw on the movie screens, the characters played by Monica Vitti, say, in *L'Avventura*, or characters in fiction, Joyce's Anna Livia Plurabelle, who had not so much a body as a flittering spirit about whom the narrator chanted, expounded, emoted, sighed in slurred words that caught my hungry ear and held it, or the seductive figure of Mangan's sister—never named—in Joyce's story "Araby," or the dispirited Madame Bovary, confused, desperate, and as hungry to give herself as I was to receive the kind of giving she proposed. Even Dante's Beatrice, though it was never young girls who attracted me. But the spirit and force of the love was something I understood that I lacked and desired.

Not that I deserved to be loved for who I was, a dark volley of hesitations and aggressions, a mystery to myself that hid beneath a layer of posturings and received habits. I was probably an attraction to certain kinds of women, the ones who want to feel thrashed by love, or wounded, or whose wounds lie so far beneath the scar tissue that they think they are nurses rather than patients. I could play all the parts I needed to play in order to entice these women and never feel I was being anything but myself. I felt excited, I felt nervous, I felt disappointed, I felt satisfaction. I was a dashing mock-heroic sad sack. Was I just raw and untutored? ill-mannered? destructive in the way that a young beast is destructive, out of instinct rather than design? Yes, that, too.

Several evenings a month my mother would call me in my shabby digs on Grand Street, Little Italy.

"Hello?"

"Hello, it's Mother."

"I recognized your voice."

"At least you recognize me."

"What does that mean, Ma?"

"Your father and I haven't seen you in so long we wouldn't recognize you."

"Sure you would."

"I'm not so sure. Ever since you came back from Europe, you've been a stranger around here."

"You mean I'm strange?"

"Not strange. A stranger. We never see you unless we come in for a visit."

"Would you like to come in?"

"We'd like to see you, yes."

"So when would you like to come?"

"When would we like? We would like you to invite us."

"Mom, you're invited."

"For when?"

"Sunday," I said. "Why not Sunday?"

"Why not Sunday? You tell me why not."

So they would come of a Sunday, bearing large quantities of food she had prepared for me at home, a charming Old World custom that as a son of the New World I could scarcely abide.

"Why are you bringing all this to me?"

"Why? We want you to have something to eat when you're hungry."

"When I'm hungry, I eat," I said. "You don't have to worry."

"Look at the kitchen," she said. "If you can call this little shelf a kitchen. What do you have here?"

"It's an efficiency," I said.

"You can be efficient, and have nothing." She studied the dust-kittens rippling across the floor.

"Listen to your mother," my father said, staring at the kitchen space as though he had never seen anything like it before. "I was your age, I didn't eat right. I know what it's like." He gave me a long searching look, and I wondered just how much he did know about the way I was living. It should be nothing, because I told him nothing. I had built a wall between us. Or a dam. Family life was like a thickly tangled skein, or a difficult knot of cord, and they wanted to keep it that way while I wanted to cut the thing in half with a sword and break free. They were old, I was young; they were Europe, I was America; they were uncomprehending, I was aware. They were prisoners of their life together; I made my own freedom. It was sometimes lonely, yes, and confusing, too, I told myself, but it was liberating me from the old New Jersey ties.

Indian summer, with its illusion of continuing warmth, passed as quickly as it arrived. And while reveling in my new freedom I fell into a thicket of complication and desire, holding out my hands to be bound like a prisoner on his way to the executioner's block.. On a night when the temperature seemed to bow toward the coming winter, I went to a party on West Thirteenth Street in an apartment that belonged to someone I'd known in college whom I had recently encountered at the chess boards in the park.

He had invited someone who had invited someone who had invited someone. It was my wife-to-be. Our eyes met, we touched hands, danced, left our coats behind and walked out into the cold night toward my street. She was witty and smart, pretty, jazzy, keen to come with me. Only when we reached my apartment did I discover just how drunk we were. I paid no attention, taking advantage of her—taking advantage of myself.

In the light of a late October morning her red hair and her pure-pale skin gave off a penumbra of scarlet, as though she glowed from beneath her skin. During the next few weeks we saw each other as much as her school schedule would allow. Her weekends in the city began on Thursdays and ended on Tuesdays. The dean of students at her college quickly saw through the ruse she had employed—the address of a friend in the city—and found my telephone number, because of my recent graduation from the same university. One night the telephone rang, and the dean asked for her. I said I hadn't seen her, but in such a way that only a fool would have believed me. Tell her, the caller said to me, that she had better come to my office immediately.

The next afternoon the dean told her that she was going on probation and that her parents would be notified at once.

This gloriously smart young woman knew how to respond to such a declaration. Her father was an Air Force officer and she had spent her childhood and early adolescence finding ways to show him he was not *her* commander. She immediately left school and came to stay with me. And then went back again. That was the neurotic rhythm of that span of days. Meanwhile my friends from Spain moved back to New Jersey and found what they described as a beautiful little house on the Millstone River only a few miles southwest of New Brunswick where we had all gone to school. I was going to take my new red-haired flame there one weekend in November when the call came from my father.

I WAS LYING there on my bed in the apartment staring at the brick wall, at the dust-kittens, when my father told me in a teary quavering voice about what had happened in Dallas. I listened to what he said, his droning voice giving me the grievous news that seemed so personal and yet so distant, so remote and yet so overwhelming.

"I came here for *this?*" he said over and over again. "I left Russia to escape the oppression, and now I hear *this?*" He talked of Czars and pogroms, of Old Country killings, the assassinations of dukes and kings. "I hoped you would never know anything like this," he said in a wail. "I hoped you would never know this . . ."

I wasn't sure what he meant, except that I could feel something similar to what he must have felt, the shock, the patriotic grief.

"Come home," he said in the saddest way I had ever heard him speak. He sounded so lonely, and I thought to myself, has something else happened? Has something happened to my mother? Is he all alone in the house? Only years later—perhaps just now as I write this—did I understand that the sadness I heard was that of a man hurt to tears by history, by the personal impersonal, by the grand confusion of all that surrounds us.

I hung up the telephone and dashed downstairs, ran out of the building. On Grand Street, people were gathering on the sidewalks, in the street, standing about the street corners, shaking their heads, waving, wringing their hands. The noise was rising. Someone in the family had gone, all of a sudden. Maybe someone else in the family had done the deed, as well! Shouts and wails!

My new flame and I were supposed to meet at the bus station later in the afternoon. At our rendezvous we both understood that we couldn't go back to the apartment, not just yet. And so we spent the evening wandering about the city, stopping in at corner bars on the Upper East Side, and then in the Village, drinking slowly, and watching the unfolding of the terrible news on television screens all over the city.

You know the story, the trip to Dallas, the motorcade, the shots, his head exploding from the force of the bullet, his wife scrambling onto the boot of the limousine, the race to the hospital, the announcement of his death, the swearing in of a new President, and all of our separate stories attached to this singular event. His story. Your story. Her story. My story. This story of how the weekend elapsed, as we then decided to take the bus across the river and visit my friends in New Jersey. Jim met us at the bus station in New Brunswick, wearing as somber a face as any of the people on the streets in New York. I knew that he wasn't happy about having returned to the United States, and the killing of the President deepened his personal grief.

"It's all coming down," he said.

I didn't have to ask what.

He and Renate had rented a small two-story cottage on the east bank of the Millstone River. As soon as we arrived we went inside to watch the somber events unfold on the television screen. As the funeral preparations began, my new love and I clung to each other on the sofa, and when we went outside for a walk along the river we moved unsteadily, as though the other person were another half of a single body that might fall away if either of us lessened our grasp.

The river ran sluggishly south, dark brown to the point of opacity. Jim said he'd heard from his landlord that snakes swam past this point in summer. The fresh-water essence of the slow-moving water rose to our nostrils, even on this cool late autumn afternoon giving off a distinctive and slightly rotting perfume.

2. BODIES OF WATER

A glimpse of him wrapped in white cloth in the small room off the main sanctuary of the mortuary. Who is this man? Who was? I saw all of the folks—family, friends, strangers to me, though my first wife was there with our son and I was grateful for that, instantly grateful.

His body—the body—wrapped in white. Chinese color of mourning. Also, Egyptian tinge to things, the whiteness of the swaddling clothes. Proximity of birth and death. And the way he had spoken of his Russian infancy, the memorable image he conjured up of the child wrapped in many layers of cloth for winter, never to be unbound until the weather warmed. Here he was again, wrapped for the long cold season.

The body swaddled in white. Wheeled out in its coffin now to be displayed before us. White for mourning. White for winter. Snows of that cold season, water in the lakes frozen, ice forming at the river banks with only a small channel running down the center of the stream beds, if running at all. Out of my body my mind lifted me, floating over the hall, over the roof, over the town, out and south past New Brunswick to the curling run of the Millstone River, frozen now in this January, and all the waters of his native Russia freezing even deeper in my heart.

I HAD BEEN standing in the shower, my arms upraised to the gush of water from the nozzle, when my wife—my second wife—poked her head in the door to the bathroom and called my name. An early morning summons to the telephone. My brother on the line.

I stared out the bedroom window at the dormant redbud trees that marked the back line of our property, the ditch filled with frozen water. I had traveled some, spent time in Europe and Mexico, returned north, and then came south, to this city in east Tennessee where winter did not feel much like a raw season to someone who had grown up in New Jersey. Twenty years, two marriages, three children, two of whom were still asleep in a room at the other side of the hallway. We'd explain to them that I had to leave that afternoon to attend a funeral.

First, I had some work to do. A book review for the *New York Times*. Yes, they'll say, the day of his father's death, he wrote a book review before he left for the funeral. But I couldn't yet weep—that would take a long, long time—and the airplane didn't leave for some hours. So I sat down and wrote the review, changed my clothes, went to the bank.

My wife reports that while she was sitting in the car waiting for me at the bank, a black woman came out, looked at her, and said, "That your man in there? You better get him out!" It had something to do with identification. I needed to cash a check for my trip but I hadn't brought along my bank ID card. The teller said I needed it. I shouted at her that my father had died and that I needed the money to get to his funeral. The guard turned around, touched his fingertips to the grip of his weapon. I shouted again that I needed the money and I needed it now. My wife came into the bank just then, and as she always could do at the worst of times, settled me down and led me out the door and returned to complete the transaction herself.

I flew north that afternoon seated next to an executive from a new telephone company who explained to me over the course of the flight the advantages of optical fiber and the future of telecommunications. My father's dead, I kept telling myself, but I also found myself listening intently to the man's rap about phones. My brother met me at Newark Airport in tears, but I didn't cry on the ride to my parents' house. My grief lay frozen inside me.

Wearing a stone face, I plunged into the house full of mourners. For hours I stood close to my mother while she told her story, over and over to anyone who asked and to anyone who didn't.

"I woke up in the middle of the night, maybe it was two-thirty in the morning. He was breathing funny. He'd had a cold for several days. 'You want some tea?' I said to him, 'Some tea might be good.' He shook his head. 'Tea will keep me up,' he said. But then a minute later he said, 'Maybe I'll have some tea after all.' So I go to fix him his tea. It's dark. It's cold in the house. Winter in the night. You know, we turn the heat down at night. It's healthier. So I went down to the kitchen to fix his tea and when I brought it back to him he was sitting up waiting for it. He coughed a little cough, he smiled at me. I sat next to him, like I was the mother and he was the child, and I offered him some tea—it was Lipton, with a half a table-spoon of honey, the way he likes it—and he sipped from the spoon. 'Ah,' he makes a noise in his throat, as if he's enjoying the taste. I spooned up a little more for him, and I remember I was thinking to myself, 'Isn't it some-thing, it's just like I was the mother and he was the child, mother and child all over again.' And he sipped this next spoonful of tea, and again he made that noise, that 'Ah,' and then he just stopped. The liquid dribbled down his chin. His lips closed, his throat closed. His eyes closed. He was gone."

The house crowded with relatives, neighbors, friends, strangers. My mother's voice rising above the babble, telling her story. Only at night did she calm down. I slept uncomfortably, in my parents' house, not the house where I had grown up. Lying in the dark, I thought of revolutionary new communication equipment, miles and miles of optical fiber, the country, the world connected with all these lines. Lines underground, lines beneath mountains, under oceans, crossing rivers.

"I woke up in the middle of the night," she was saying to someone on the telephone the next morning. She seemed to be moving through the day as if it were a dream, telling her story over and over again.

"Mother," I said. "Take your mind off this particular point."

She stared at me as though I had cursed her soundly.

"It's important to me," she said.

"Please," I said. "You must have other things on your mind. Don't torture yourself."

"It's too soon not to torture myself," she said.

But the next morning she sat at the kitchen table, before any of the family, friends, neighbors would arrive, and looking like an unfeathered bird, her eyes raw with the work of crying through the night, she said, "I listened to what you told me. When I was trying to get to sleep, I tried to remember other things. I remembered some."

"What, Ma?"

"This cold weather, I was thinking, I remembered one winter when I was a very small child, it was so cold, never before was it so cold, and the river froze all the way out almost to the bay, and my mother bundled up me and my brother and put us on a sled, just like the Old Country, and pulled us on the ice all the way to the lighthouse."

"Amazing, Ma," I said. "I don't remember anything from when I was that young."

"You have to get older to remember the early things," she said.

"Do you?" I said.

"Yes, and I remembered something else."

"Tell me."

"I remembered when I was a little baby, just born, and my mother took me to her mother's house and they gave me a milk bath."

"A milk bath?"

"Water wasn't good enough. She bathed me in milk. For my skin. So you think that's why today I have such a good complexion?"

She made a little laugh, and I tried to laugh, but couldn't.

"You were just an infant and you remember this?"

"It came to me. I remember it. I've always remembered it."

"I'm glad," I said. "It's a lovely thing to think about. Especially right now."

Tears came to her eyes.

"I'll think about what I want to think about," she said.

At the funeral I stood before his white-swathed body at the mortuary—he seemed so pale, had they bathed him in milk?—catching my breath, preparing to speak.

"He was a good man," I said. Mumble, mumble, keeping back the tears. I had things prepared. Then came visions of his life, the life he led as a young man—younger than I was at this moment—in Russia, his days in the Red Air Force, dashing young officer, all that, then his misadventure that led him to Japan, to China, finally across the Pacific to Hawaii—"a Paradise," he called it, "you should only have seen it then!"—then to San Francisco, and a train ride across the country to Brooklyn, where he met my mother at a dance at a social hall.

Words left me, words came to me, words not my own.

"He rests," I said. "He is weary," I said. "He has traveled."

3. LUCKY STONES

Running toward the low-lapping waves on the stony beach where the Raritan River meets the salt-water bay. Ten years old or maybe a year or two younger, younger brother in tow, father behind, up near the boardwalk. Bending to search for the brown smooth ovoid stones to pitch out onto the surface of the water. Here's one, pick it up, feel its satiny finish under the fingers, pull your arm back, ready, then sling the stone out over the waves. And if you're lucky, see it hop, skip, across the surface, sometimes one hop, sometimes two. As far as I could throw the stone and make it skim, that was how far I could imagine the breadth of the world, that was how far I could imagine distance in time.

Skimming along over the surface, what a way to live!

4. PLOW

Snowy night, winding roads of southwestern Vermont, late nineteen-seventies, my son asleep in the house back in Bennington, my new wife—my second—and I bundled up and driving along the frozen roads in our blue Volkswagen beetle. White, all's white aswirl around us, sliding on the curves of the country highway, feeling as though we could have been at sea, sailing directly into high white waves, as we were driving.

My wife had gone into labor some hours before, and despite the cold my brow broke out in sweat and sweat trickled down the underside of my arms. I drove leaning as close to the windshield as possible, fearing that the small wipers could not push the heavy wet snow back much longer.

"Oh," she had said when her water broke about a half hour before we climbed into the car.

My own voice now, echoing that sigh.

"Are you all right?" she said.

"Am I? Are you?"

"Can you see?"

"Not great. But I'll get us there."

Midnight now, and not another car in sight, only the strange dark expanse of countryside glowing with the luminescence of white snow against dimness of night, a bluish light, as though we were moving through a dark room in the afterglow of a fire. Or moonglow without the presence of the moon. Or the radiation of the earth itself, particles of rock and tree and snow and cloud giving off an essence of interior vitality we would never notice during the day.

"We're sliding," she said, her voice hushed because of the intensity of her contractions.

"I'm doing my best," I said, fearing that in this instance my best, if that was what I was doing, was not enough. The snow seemed to be turning to frozen water, and our little vehicle behaved as much like a small boat or a water-sled as a car. My worst fear blew up on the window before me, a picture of us sliding into a ditch and getting stuck there while she went into full labor.

The winds blew harder, the wipers ceased to work, and the window almost instantly filled up with snow, blocking my view entirely. I slowed down, fearful of stopping completely because I did not know that I could work up enough traction beneath the tires to start moving again. Rolling my window down I leaned out of the car and reached forward and around with my left hand as far as I could and tried to brush the ice from the windscreen.

Down in the valley of the shadow of the snow, we pushed forward into the freeze, my hand becoming as numb as my mind. The normal twenty-minute drive from house to hospital—we had clocked it many a time during our birth-training classes there—had already stretched into over an hour, and it seemed as though we had gone scarcely half the distance. I don't know how we made it the rest of the way. The snow fell harder and harder, and when the wind slashed it across the front of the little car it surged in through the open window, splashing onto the left side of my face, down my left shoulder and into my lap.

"It's cold," she said in a strained voice, drawing out the word into a moan.

"I know," I said, breathing carefully, almost as though I were going into labor myself. "I know it is. I know."

"Keep going," she said. "We can't stop."

"I know," I said. "I know. I know."

She was a brave determined woman, the kind of woman—I knew before this moment but understood it full well in my bones just then—who might have gone west in a covered wagon and hacked out a sod-house from the sloping prairie and made it a place for herself and her family to live, giving birth every year to another child, mastering the arts of frontier survival, perhaps even taking up a rifle and making the kill for the family's meals. In the next few minutes she scarcely made a sound, just the raspy noise of her increasingly more powerful breathing. My own breathing became harsh with strain and worry as the snow blew across the front of the car with even greater force, and the open highway took on more and more of the aspect of the open sea in storm.

Then suddenly the lights of the village appeared dimly ahead, blurring in and out of my vision as the wind swept the snow before the tall streetlamps of Cambridge, New York. I slowed down and steadied our course on the roadway. The path opened up, a plow, a plow had just carved out the route.

The streets became even more intensely white as we approached the hospital hill, a gently rising slope atop which rested Mary McClellan, a former TB sanatorium turned into a modern hospital when the region had grown after World War Two. The plow had done the streets, so I drove fearlessly now as my wife breathed carefully alongside me, certain that since the hill was steep enough to worry about it would be one of the first roads plowed in a storm. Then we turned the corner, only to see a wide unbroken swath of snow. I swallowed hard and increased our speed, following the New England rule of accelerating to go uphill in order to avoid losing traction midway.

"What?" my wife said.

"You all right?"

"They're coming closer together," she said.

"Breathe," I said. I was breathing myself.

And pushing my foot onto the gas pedal while holding steady to the wheel as we began our ascent in the deep wet snow lined by dark rows of pines, snow that seemed to turn to ice as we rammed our way uphill. Certain that we were going to have to make it without help, I leaned further over the wheel, keen to spy out any possible obstructions—fallen tree or stalled vehicle—as focused as I had ever been on keeping this little car moving. Midway, as we turned a gentle curve and began yet another increment of the climb, blinding lights came up quickly behind us.

The plow! We had beaten the plow by a minute or so in the race up the hill. Who would have imagined we could have beaten the plow!

But the machine gained rapidly on us so that in another few seconds I had to steer to the right or risk getting rammed, and we slid into the snow and ditch as the plow sped by us, spraying more heavy wet snow onto our vehicle. As a child that's bundled up in winter finds that another blanket has just been piled on top of it and so lapses comfortably into a deep night's sleep, our little car gave a shudder and stalled out, settling deeper under its cover of snow, unable to move even if I could have started it again.

I looked at my wife and she looked at me. Her face seemed relaxed in the ghostly light of the road lamp and snow fell thickly behind the window behind her as if to frame the serenity of her face.

I listened for a moment to the mannered hiss of her labored breathing and said, "We've got to walk."

The hardest part of our struggle was getting out of the car. Snow had packed against the doors on my side, and on hers the car had pushed right up against a snow bank that masked the ditch. After a minute or so of shoving my weight against my door, I managed to push it open enough for me to insert myself like a wedge and force the door open wider. I climbed out and shoveled snow with my bare hands to free the door enough for her—after she slowly and carefully climbed over the gear shift in a quiet and pantomimic action that belied her labor and made me think of a slow-motion dance on film—so that she could step out into the snow.

Hand in hand we started up the hill.

The wind blew the snow sideways across our faces, slanting it in toward the ditch side of the road, making our way seem all aslant itself, as though we were struggling uphill in a bowl some giant hand kept turning in order to keep the snow flowing down and across our path.

"How are you doing?" I asked her as we took large strides up the road, swinging our arms in long arcs, taking in deep gulps of the cold snowy air, more like two adolescents marching along on a warm day in early spring than the pair of worried adults we were.

"All right," she said, through teeth tightly clenched. No pack or weight could have burdened a hiker more than the throes of her contractions worried my wife right now. But she kept moving along with me, good trouper that she was, carrying our unborn child like baggage.

"It's about a mile, maybe less," I said, remembering the distance when we drove it to our last birthing class. Up another couple of hundred yards and then another turn in the road and then another long climb before another tilting to the right—the way seemed so much longer than our entire drive before. One foot after another, in boots, in heavy coats, the air cold and dense, the wind pushing against us as it shifted its direction, shoveling snow straight at our faces, into our frost-hooded eyes: we moved along and up, along and up, two people, resembling a primeval couple, battling their way through a storm in order to bring a child to the light.

Light! All around us the trees glowed and the snow shined and the wind blew, and our breath spewed out in a ghostly phosphorescence, torn away at once by the wailing wind. We were two creatures of another order, walking beneath the depths of a great ocean or deep deep lake; our motion slowed when we reached the next bend in the road and a great gush of wind rolled down upon us like an avalanche or a spumy ocean wave.

We pressed ahead, dizzy with our burden and our goal, reaching out now to gulp huge breaths of air like swimmers making their way forward under great pressure beneath the sea. Up and up, our chests heaving with breath, she with her heavy burden, and me with my goal of getting us there safely, in time to make all go well.

And then the light increased. Lights! The tall lamps of the hospital parking lot, and a nurse bundled into a thick winter parka rushing toward us pushing a wheelchair.

"You called," she said, nearly breathless herself, "and then you didn't arrive!"

I began to recount the story of our travels, from the ice-slick road to the part where the plow buried us, but she was already busy helping my wife into the chair and turning her around in the snowbound lot and rolling her toward the entrance to the building now no more than a hundred yards away.

Labor went both quickly, and slowly. My wife breathed her special breaths when the contractions ceased, rolled with them when they came again. I stood next to her, recording them in a little notebook. As I wrote I recalled the old Hebrew myth that on the High Holidays God Himself inscribes your name for the coming year, depending on your goodness and devotion, in either the fabled Book of Life or the dreaded Book of Death.

This little notebook was my own Book of Life.

> *1 a.m. contract., 1 min.*
> *1:03 a.m. contract., 1 min.*
> *1:06 a.m. contract., 1 min.*

She breathed, huffed and puffed the proper rhythms, and then rolled again with the contractions, her body itself become the sea, with its tidal waves and ebbings, and her spirit, and our small child almost to be, both riders upon it.

> *3:22, contr., 2 min.*
> *3:34, contr., 2 min.*
> *3:36, contr., 2 min.*

It was quiet in the labor room except for her breathing, her breathing and mine.

> *4:37, con. 2*
> *4:39, con. 2*
> *5:01, c., 1*
> *5:49, c. 2 . . .*

Time contracted to a small space, as did the rest of the world. Once in the middle of all this I remembered the snow, pictured it falling hard, blown aslant across the treescape, across the road, white chains of snow flowing into the dark of the wooded hillside. Then time brought me back to the moment, to the place, the space of my life, to the place where life begins. A woman, breathing hard, her cervix dilating, the beginning of everything, woman alone, the man to the side, obedient though not servile to the rhythm of the coming event. As in war when a woman might stand by her partner and pass him his weapon so that he might thrust and slam and cleave the enemy, so now I stepped aside to let this wave rush past, and allow her to take over the occasion.

Light came up around us as we moved—rolled—to the delivery room. Light splashed over us, the hot lamps on the ceiling bearing down on this small room, this narrow bed. This joyous moment, all we lacked for it was music. But we had the sounds of voices, the nurses talking, coaching, cheering, the doctor rushing in, breathing hard, talking of the heavy snow, and my own breathing which now that I had others around I could hear as a hoarse and insistent music of its own in counterpoint to my wife's stream of sound.

Came the outcry of my first daughter!

Light spewed in through the windows as bright red blood splashed about the white white room, splattering on the nurses' smocks, on the walls, almost, it seemed, passing through the wide glass of the large windows that showed us the surrounding hills all white—bright white—as early dawn light seemed to seep up through the snow itself. Winter water, the sea water turned to fallen snow, the bright red blood—these colors made an emblem of the morning.

5. IN THE "Y" POOL

Afternoons in summer, returning from the woodsy camp site, piling out of the buses where we had sung ourselves hoarse, into the cool housing of the "Y," down the stairs to the basement lockers, undressing quickly, wondering what it was like on the girls' side of the locker room, these thoughts soon lost as we shuffle barefoot over the wet tiles into the shower room, douse ourselves with tepid water, then pass into the underground area of the pool, lining up to dive into the warm chlorine-laced waters.

Diving down, down to touch the slippery tiles at the bottom, holding our breaths, holding, holding in the air, chests burning, lungs on fire, waiting to see who'll be the last to float to the surface . . . eyes closed, knees to chest, hanging there in the water, like a dead man . . .

6. TELLING AND SINGING

For Josh, my firstborn, Manhattan infant, Mexico bound, a story. About a man named Fadouley who wore many hats.

Once upon a time there was a man named . . .

At bedtime we'd sit in the dark, young man and young boy, laying out this serial tale, words as stepping stones toward sleep. Sweet male child, my words to his ears.

For daughter Emma, more than ten years later in the midst of a Vermont snowstorm, curled up in a kittenish shape on my chest, I sang,

> *Has there ever been a girl like Emma*
> *In the whole wide history of the world?*
> *No—there's never been!*

Sonya. My last-born. Coming into the world on a hot day in late July, New England heat wave. Jaundiced. Two extra days in the hospital.

I made up a song for her.

> *Sonya,*
> *No one'll ever own ya,*
> *But they'll always telephone ya,*
> *You're my little Sonya Ruth*
> *And that's the truth.*

Each of them I bathed. Each of them I laved. (I like that word enormously. A luxurious bathing is what it conjures for me. Laved.) Laving. Bathing. The preparation of the young body for sleep. As they grow, they begin to bathe themselves. One day, they decide to shower. And in the morning. Time turned around. Oh, the water that has poured down on them, splashed across their beautiful bodies!

7. TO THE LIGHTHOUSE

Her frozen breath rising straight up into the still air. Poised at the shore that seemed no longer a shore but rather like a rug leading down to a strange cracked and splintered floor of white and off-white.

"Mama," she said, not knowing whether to be frightened or merely mystified as she watched her breath turn to motes of crystal.

"Hush," her mother says. Big broad dark-haired woman, bundled in a fur, her wide lips chapped from the cold. Eyes like beacons, searching the horizon. Far out along the ice small dark figures twitched along the seam where the sky met the frozen river.

"Where are we going, Mama?"

"I've always wanted," the big woman said, taking her by the hand.

"What, Mama?"

"Walk, darling," her mother said.

And so they started forward, leaving the beach behind them, stepping over the heaps of frozen water that lay like dirty dinner plates stacked haphazardly in a sink. They struggled mightily to walk a hundred feet. But once beyond these obstacles the ice turned as smooth as a dance floor and she walked ahead of her mother, deliberately sliding and slipping along. The sun was bright, but gave off no heat. It reminded her of the small light bulb in the pantry which she sometimes thought about as she lay in bed at night trying to fall asleep.

"See," her mother said, pointing with her mittened hand toward the lighthouse that marked the spot where the river met the bay.

The lighthouse white against the white of the ice, the pale-white of the sky beyond; and the gray line of the south bank of the river; and when she turned around, the wooded shore of Staten Island, and turning further, the sight of their own beach, like a rotogravure, the houses etched into the air behind it.

Had they walked that far already? Halfway from the beach, halfway to the lighthouse. She hadn't known she was that strong, weighed down by heavy coat and leggings, to walk so far in this cold air, picking up one fat leg after another. The sun. Yet no heat.

"Mama?"

"We're almost there," her mother said.

When they arrived, their neighbors, the Greenberg twins, were racing around and around on the ice! Mrs. Klein from the butcher shop, holding her young daughter in her arms, gazing back at the shoreline. Abe Rasmussen, the fishmonger, teaching his three boys how to skate. And others, mostly strangers, bundled against the cold, sliding along on the ice, or staring up past the rocks at the base of the lighthouse. Smiling at her when she approached. It was like a dream of winter, because the river had never frozen before within the span of anyone's recollection.

8. WATER BUGS AND VIOLINS

Glimpses of water and rocks, the view out toward where the bay meets the ocean.

Water bugs larger than my thumbs racing across the wooden floor of the small living room in the second-floor apartment next to the dairy.

Simon's Dairy—early morning rumbling of trucks delivering cannisters of milk, later the delivery trucks head out, carrying their commercial load to stores around the town.

Water and milk, rocks and insects. These are my earliest recollections.

Earlier in childhood I believed that I had flown in an airplane, but later I realized that I had seen a photograph my parents had taken while flying (from New York to Washington, D.C., I think it was, just after they had gotten married) and in my childlike way had assumed that I had been there with them on that flight.

My first full memories, full, as in a scene in a story or a film, come to me of evenings in another second-story apartment which I spent with my mother's father. He was a frail, white-haired man, about five-foot six or seven, who wore an old gray pinstriped suit and played the violin. He had a patch over one eye—left or right I can't say for sure—and a wolflike smile. Because he and my grandmother owned a tobacco and candy store on the town's main street he always arrived with his suit pockets full of sweets.

While my parents went out to a movie, he stayed with me and my brother, often playing the violin for us while we hummed on our make-shift instruments made of combs and tissue paper.

"Ta-ta-ta-ta-taaay-ta, ee-ee-ee-uh . . ."

The Hebrew National Anthem was our main number. But sometimes we branched out to "Old McDonald Had a Farm" and "Sweet Mystery of Life."

"Tah-tee tah-tee tah-tee tah-tee tah-tee-ta . . ."

We would already have eaten supper, and the candy bars served as a wonderful dessert. When it came time, our faces smeared with chocolate and our bellies full, we gladly bathed and changed into our pajamas and climbed into our beds, while our grandfather slid his bow across the strings of the violin a few more swipes, humming as he played, making music our entry into the time of sleep.

I rarely dreamed. But now and then I had a dream so vivid I believed I was awake. It would have me sitting up in bed and leaning to the right, staring straight through the open bedroom door and across the kitchen into the pantry where the comic strip figure of Krazy Kat, his pointy ears jutting out like weapons, darted back and forth, in and out of the pantry.

I feared this critter. What danger? what punishment might he inflict? I didn't know but he worried me. For years I wondered if some action of mine might bring down on me the wrath of Krazy Kat.

9. THE NEW WORLD

Out beyond this beach where I often played as a child you can see the beginning of the curve—periplum—and imagine how all this once made a paradise, deer walking down to the waterside, lapping quietly at the base of trees where the fresh water pooled after the tide pulled back, turning their heads now and then at the splash of a wave.

Otters dived for clams in the old bay, making small wakes. Sunlight, spring and summer heat nourished multiplicities of plants. Small animals chewed at the roots, birds pecked at seeds. Nothing vast had occurred here for thirty million years, all this land sloping gently toward the water. To the west, a river flowed out of very old hills, but here it bled away into marshes before lapsing into the bay.

On the sand, horseshoe crabs, looking like catchers' mitts on legs, walked sidewise toward each other to mate or do battle, and past the spit of land ranged large schools of fish. Imagine the peace, a million years of it at least, of only animal noise and occasional thunderstorms, the wind in the tree branches, the boom and crack and lightning hiss of rain above the trees, the wash of waves in winter winds, the snap and crack of ice in the coldest part of winter.

All these years, this point of land displayed no special beauty, only the tranquility of its solitude. From earthworm to owl, from roots to topmost leaves, it was young and it was ancient, it was spare and yet a miracle of spectacle in miniature in the plenitude of small creation: this particular point of land that had no name because no one lived here to speak one.

10.   KISMET

I don't remember much about the musical itself, except that it was my first trip to Broadway. Our Temple chorus—all of us teenagers—went as a group. On the train in from Perth Amboy, I sat one seat behind the girl who was my first real crush.

Dancers with deerlike legs, their bodies draped in golden gauze and silvery silks whirling about the stage while violins sizzled and tambourines jingled and saxophones crooned in baritone melodies I never dared to sing except when I was alone and thinking about this girl. Harem guards slashed the air with gleaming scimitars, and a powerful man with a long pointy beard sang to a young woman with hair as dark as my room at home in the middle of a moonless winter night.

At the end of the show we went backstage. Our music director knew a man in music publishing who was also part of the male singer's entourage.

"Look at them," one of my friends said as we threaded our way past groups of weary, half-naked female dancers who slumped against flats and exposed water pipes, whispering like teachers on a cigarette break. They smelled of face cream and sweat and smoke and had small breasts and up close their legs seemed more sturdy than beautiful.

At an unmarked door just off the far side of the stage, the music director tapped a few erratic knocks.

A weary voice told us to come in.

In the small dressing room stood the bearded star who on stage had sung about Paradise. He was of medium height and wore an old blue bathrobe and we could see the collar of his undershirt beneath it.

"Hello, boys and girls," he said, his tired eyes wandering toward the illuminated mirror behind the dressing table in which we were all reflected in the harsh light of naked bulbs. The girl I was mad for stared back at me in the glass from where she stood just at the singer's shoulder.

"Is that real?" I heard myself say.

Before anyone could stop me, I pushed my way forward, grabbed the man's pointy beard and yanked so hard he yowled like a dog.

11. DEAD SEA

The white-skinned, hairless, enormously fat bald man floated on his back in the water, a slim band of dark suit cutting across the middle of his otherwise naked body. Motionless, he floated. No movement of arms or legs. His eyes closed. Hot sun burning down on him. No wind. White surface of the water unmarred by waves or currents. He looked like a strange, inedible variety of discarded vegetation.

On the shore several children sang to themselves some nonsense song in Hebrew, or perhaps the Hebrew just sounded like nonsense. I stood there in my shorts, shirtless, feeling the sun bear down on my neck, shoulders, arms, chest.

"Will you go in?" said the girl standing next to me. "What are you waiting for?"

We had driven in from the farm—the kibbutz—where I was staying, working in the tomato fields, weeding—knee-burning, back-straining work. This tanned freckle-faced Sabra with a single blonde braid that trailed down her back nearly to her waist lived and worked on the kibbutz; she had told me that if I did anything on my first free afternoon it should be to swim in the Dead Sea.

"You will never forget," she said.

"You must go," my father had said over the telephone when I had called home from Athens with a question about my draft status.

"I must?" I said.

"You must go there. It's your heritage. All the years I struggled in the Soviet Union—"

"You didn't struggle," I said. "You were an officer in the Red Air Force. You lived a life of privilege."

"Before I went to the Air Force Academy it was a struggle. Our family scraped and scrimped. We lived among all the anti-Semites. I had to fight my way through school."

"But then you became an officer."

"Even then I had my runarounds with—"

"You mean run-ins?"

"Run-ins," he said. "Run-ins with the no-goodniks. Why, I remember..."

I reminded him that this was a transatlantic call. No more stories.

"Hello?" My mother had taken the telephone at the New Jersey end of the line.

"Hello, Ma," I said.

"You didn't write. We were worried."

"I'm fine," I said. And I was fine. Though when I had left Spain for Italy, I had not been fine, having picked up some nasty infection from an excursion to a certain house in Málaga. But then I was fine again. And then in Belgrade I had not been fine, staying there in the middle of the winter with terrible bronchitis, nursed back to health by a wizened old woman, my landlady, who nourished me with hot tea and lemon every hour through a week of awful nights. Now I was fine again.

"Your father will send you the money," she said, lowering her voice, as though it were possible—I doubted it—that he could not hear what she was saying. "He wants you to go. Go for him, will you, please?"

The next day he wired the cash for a boat ticket to Haifa. I bought a ticket on a Greek steamer that left from Piraeus in a couple of days. I had been to the port about a week or so before to visit a brothel that my host, a school chum named Ron Geller, said was the original of the brothel in the film *Never on Sunday*. Our visit brought us to a dimly lighted one-story house with a number of small rooms and four or five listless young women—all dark, none of them blonde like the ancient Greeks I had read about in college. No one looked like Melina Mercouri.

"It must be another place," Geller said. "Let's go." He wanted to continue his search but I wanted to return to Athens to try to find an English nurse whom I had met at a party some nights before. Neither of us had much luck that night. When I returned to Piraeus to board that steamer I asked the cab driver if he knew which of the brothels was the model for the whorehouse in the movie.

He turned to me and shrugged.

I found my ship. On board I met an Israeli couple who when they learned I had no fixed destination said I must visit their daughter at the kibbutz near the Dead Sea.

"A charming place," the elderly man said. "Unique in Israel, unique perhaps in all the world."

"Don't exaggerate," his wife said. "He'll see what he sees."

Passage across the Mediterranean, like sailing across a huge blue lake.

Tel Aviv reminded me of the sun-drenched, down-at-heels beach town of Asbury Park, New Jersey, a place I knew well from my childhood and high school days. After a few days, I took a bus south toward the Negev Desert, stopping to spend a night in Beersheba. The market there gave me a little thrill, with Bedouin leading camels into the narrow lanes of the marketplace, the high pyramids of fresh fruit, the winey odors of coffee and figs and various sorts of burning incense and the air filled with the gargle and hisses of languages I understood not at all. I ate in the market and wandered through the odd halls of a new shopping mall directly across the road, and imagined the camels stepping through the plate glass doorway of the deserted modern building.

That night I rented a bed in a hostel, beginning my sleep alone in the room and being awakened several times as one new roomer after another stumbled through the door and found an empty bed. By dawn the snores rose above the snuffing of the camels outside the window. Of all the inhabitants of that room I dressed first and went out into the street, finding strong coffee in the marketplace. By the time the sun had risen above the flat roofs of the town I was climbing into a bus heading southwest on a road that wound between steep declivities of desert arroyos, down and down toward the flat seabed that marked the border between Israel and Jordan.

At the kibbutz where acres of vegetables were planted in the middle of this burning desert flat, water seemed a miracle. I drank my fill and more, asked where I might bathe. The next afternoon the daughter of the couple I had met on board the steamer invited me to swim in the Dead Sea. That was how I caught sight of the fat balding man afloat on the salt surface.

After a few minutes I noticed another old man wading into the sluggish water, holding an object in each hand high above his head, his pale white body in contrast to the sepia rock and sand, the dark stones of the shoreline, the burning gold of the sky filled with sun. I looked away to the bald man and heard the sound of violin music—a loopy, whiney Eastern melody that might have come from the old Victrola in my grandparents' house back in New Jersey when I was a child. Floating on his back like the bald man, the pale slender gentleman lay atop the buoyant surface, playing his violin while the fat fellow waved his arms in accompaniment, conducting an invisible orchestra out where the body of salt water stretched into the white-hot horizon on the Jordan shore.

Suddenly the music shifted, I squinted into the sun, took a deep breath, and with the silver cadenzas of Bach sliding through the near-molten air, I stepped into the water. It felt thick and sluggish around my knees, and I paused to reconsider.

"More!" called out my freckle-faced guide.

If she hadn't been there to watch, I might have turned and walked back to shore through that water with the consistency of spoiled milk, its odor a mixture of salt and sulphur. But her cries spurred me on.

"More! More!"

Wading out to my waist.

"You Americans are cowards!" she shouted over the water.

The music swooped up and around me, turning tinny the closer I got to the floating violinist.

"More!" she called.

So I lay back on the surface, achieving that fine sensation of being held up by the densest liquid on earth, opening and closing my eyes—so that it went dark, bright, dark, brightest, brightest sun I'd ever floated beneath—while around me the violin screeched like a diving hawk as the unlikely musician segued into "The Marseillaise". . . and then "God Save the Queen," "The Battle Hymn of the Republic," "Meadowlands," and "Hatikvah" . . .

12. A DREAM?

I saw this recently, with my eyes closed, deep in a kind of meditative state. But I can't decide whether or not it is a dream or a fantasy or a vision:

From high on a mountain ridge, I'm looking down upon an extraordinary valley where a winding river shines silvery in the light of a sun high in the sky. Lush fields line both sides of the river, and at this distance, though no people are visible to the naked eye, you can see small plumes of smoke rising from a few settlements along the banks of the river. What country this is I cannot say. It reminds me of the Rocky Mountain West; it could be a piece of Europe, but then again it may be somewhere in Central Asia where this unknown river flows through this striking valley.

I lean back where I am sitting, and see that there is someone sitting next to me, cross-legged, in a long dark robe and a high conical hat, almost like a wizard's cap. It is a man, my father, and alongside him, on his left, sits another man in robe and cap, and I know, in this dream or vision or fantasy, that this man is *his* father, and next to him, another man, my great-grandfather, and on his left, along the ridge, another man and another and another, a line of forebears stretching along the ridge into which they blur, eventually becoming a smoky mark along the horizon.

A feeling of calm overtakes me. Here I sit, part of this landscape, with all of these men who have come before me.

"What is the name of this river?" I hear myself inquire.

No answer. Only the sound of the wind clutching at our robes.

"Does it have a name?"

My father turns to me, on his face the most beatific smile I have ever seen. He says nothing.

"I don't know where I am," I say. "I would like to know where I am."

Like a rush of warm water, the answer flows into my mind.

It is the river Path, the river called Path, the Path River, yes, the name comes to me, and I know that is the truth, and we will sit here and watch it at this distance, knowing that wherever it flows, it has come from some-where, wherever it comes from, it will lead further.

Another question comes to mind. And for this I have no answer.

Is this place, this high mountain ridge, this gathering of men in robes and caps the way I have come? or somewhere I am going?

Again my father smiles.

13. TRAIN ALONG THE HUDSON

When my second wife and I divorced we each moved to different cities, but I could not let go of my daughters. So my wife and I came to know each other in a new fashion—having been tortured inhabitants of a failing marriage, we became partners in a child-raising compact.

In the years after this marriage ended I drank too much and got too little sleep, ate erratically and did not take care of myself. But I made my weekend visits—and holidays, every holiday—with the girls. Looking back on it, it was not always an easy schedule to keep. But I had had practice.

When we first split up, my first wife and I, the redhead, my flaming love, she moved from our place in Vermont to New York City, taking my son with her. Night after night, during those first few weeks, I lay alone on my bed fully dressed, unable to sleep, rocking back and forth, forth and back, crying out into the dark for my boy. What made the anguish even worse was that I knew only a hundred and fifty miles or so south, Josh was suffering in the same dark night of separation.

So at least two Fridays each month, and sometimes more, throughout most of the year, for six or eight years, I would drive down to New York and pick Josh up and take him back with me to Vermont for the weekend. One weekend a month he would ride the Greyhound up to Vermont by himself. For years (he later told me) he could not abide the odor of bus fumes. The separation, wrenching him from me, tearing apart the household, lonely hours on the bus up and back, it all came back to him with the smell of the exhaust from a bus.

I don't remember much of the driving. What comes to me when I think of those years is a picture more poignant than troubling. In New Lebanon, New York, the little town we passed through after we left the Taconic Parkway on our drive north, stood a former church turned into a restaurant. Artie's, let's call it. The real name has long since slipped my mind. But I remember the warm, dimly lighted rooms in winter, good heat after the sharp and bitter cold of the air outside. On Friday nights Josh and I would stop there for supper, and on Sundays on our way back as well. Usually we had a table to ourselves. But now and then we had to sit at the bar. Muted voices all around us. Canned jazz in the background. Clink of glasses, rush of water, clank of dishes at the bar.

The boy, eight years old, sipping the hot creamy New England clam chowder from a broad spoon. The waiter delivers the steaming juicy hamburger (freshly ground from round steak in the restaurant's own kitchen) to his place at the bar.

The simplest conversation usually followed.

"How's that burger?"

"Good."

"Looks great."

"Want a bite, Dad?"

"You eat. I'll try a bite if you can't finish it."

He'd eat his burger. I had a steak—in those days we ate a great deal of red meat. And a Bloody Mary or two. And then a coffee or two.

"Dessert?"

He'd eat ice cream, usually.

I'd sip my coffee, watching him, feeling the closeness of the two of us together at the bar, our incongruous position, father and son at the bar, the boy so young and yet so at home, while the music played and the waiters served and the bartender mixed the drinks, on these winter nights in the middle of the dark of upstate New York.

So I thought to myself now and then in the early days of my separation from the girls, well, I know how to do this. And I figured that a lot of the pain would be diminished because I knew, would know, what came next. A lot of the pain the first time around came from not knowing, from living in the dark, from worrying and wondering about what would happen next.

I went about plans for visits to the girls with a certain awareness, a sense that all would be well. We would see each other at least once a month, month in and month out, and most of the holidays. Wherever I was living, I kept up those visits, traveling by car or train or airplane, whatever made the most sense at the time. As I write this, in fact, I'm riding a train from Manhattan to Albany, riding along the Hudson, following that stately river up toward the north and its Adirondack source.

In the near-decade that I've lived in Washington now, that's been my route. Early morning train up to Manhattan. Lunch with my son. (An admirable man, just past thirty, he lives and works in New York.) Then

back onto a train for the ride up the Hudson for a Friday evening reunion
with the girls, returning Sunday evening or sometimes Monday morning
on the train south. Commuting in this fashion, I've come to know the river
in several different seasons.

Riding up from Washington the train crosses the Susquehanna, the
Delaware and the Raritan, but nothing compares to the Hudson. This
river, with its wide expanse where it settles in to New York harbor, the flut-
tery icing of sails across its rippled silk waters, the great bridge that spans it
which the train rolling north passes beneath. For an hour or so you notice
the patterns made by the wind on the broad waters, imagining the Dutch
explorers who turned their bows in this same direction, making haste
toward the dim hope of the Catskills showing faintly on the horizon. You
read, you write, you doze, you dream, all the time rocked by the rattling
motion of the wheels. With eyes open you sometimes scan the surface of
the river, seeing it narrow as the cliffs rise on the Jersey side. Soldiers scaled
those rock walls during the Revolutionary War. Carters and boatmen
guided their flat barges up this route as commerce became solely American and a canal made it possible to float your cargo from here all the way
to Buffalo. The commerce has continued, though greatly diminished now.
You see mostly pleasure boats moving up and down the channel, between
the rising mountains to the west, old, old mountains, the first to appear on
this continent and the first to wear down like the lower molars of cosmic
teeth razed by constant use against the abrasive air. Well, abrasive mainly
in autumn, or at least, *bracing*. You can feel the temperature drop inside
the train car only a hundred miles north of New York City. By early
October you can see the effects of the falling temperatures, the watercolor
palette of dying—brightening—leaves.

When we lived in Vermont—my first wife and I and our son—
autumn, with all of its beautiful colors, struck me as the saddest season, pre-
figuring as it did the onset of the winter. Thousands came to admire and
sigh at the beauty of the leaves. I walked around our yard, kicking at them,
detesting what they signaled—the ice, the snow, air so cold it seemed to eat

your very lungs as you inhaled it, long dark nights, and days with the sun so weak and pathetic, like a two-watt light bulb in the sky, that it might as well be the moon.

They are beautiful though, these turning leaves, when you're only passing through and don't have to live among them. "Death is the mother of beauty," Wallace Stevens wrote. I'd modify that for a trip to New York State in the autumn. Passing through is the mother of beauty. It's a feeling resembling death, or fear of death, at least, that takes you over if you stay around to watch the leaves fall and gather on the ground, and then swirl up in great gray waves when the winds of winter begin to blow, portending the snow the wind will soon be whirling about your backyard, piling it into huge drifts that block your passage anywhere you wish to go.

Or it could be that my view of Vermont winters was a state of mind brought on by the deterioration of our marriage. When my first wife left for New York City, the weather changed in my heart, getting for a time a lot worse, and then a lot better. I met the woman who would become my second wife. My heart lightened even before the advent of spring. Despite all of the turmoil that came with a second divorce, nothing looked as bleak as it did then during those Januaries and Februaries and Marches in Vermont, three months that seemed to go on like the Ice Age itself.

Riding the river route at that time of year you observe the vast snows in layers along the cliffs and the farther north you travel the ice thickens, and finally closes over from bank to bank. You might think that the river would become a smooth road of ice. But that's not how it is. Chunks of ice brace up against each other, forming barriers to easy passage.

Past Poughkeepsie, you can see the gross signs of the change to come, in the deadening of the colors on the far mountainsides, in the dun-gathering of clouds above the river. I suppose if I were heading for the Klondike in the late eighteen hundreds I would have said to myself, well, it's going to be mighty cold up there, but that's where the gold is. Watching the frozen river I say to myself now, it's going to be mighty cold up there, but that's where my girls are living.

In order to forget about the cold I read awhile. A new novel to pass the time. Though time passes with or without it. But better with the novel. In the way that good cuisine makes nourishment more than merely palatable. Time without variation—that would be the worst torture. As in the sound of a single note, without any change above it or below. A life without variation is a life unlived. Even though the changes may bring pain. But sometimes pleasure, even happiness. The goring, bleeding bust-ups of my marriages. But along with that came the children. My life in motion, my life in stasis. No body is ever completely at rest, not even in death. The flesh rots. The bones decay. Minerals leach into the surrounding soil, or feed the fishes. In the lake. The river. The ocean.

Thinking suddenly: how to make a story out of my life until now? I know how to make a story about what I have observed around me, I know how to make a story out of situations I imagine might happen to me or other people. I know also how to make a memoir, to make pieces of an autobigraphy. But to turn the actual events that I have lived into shapely fiction? How to shape a life that is essentially unfinished until the end? Musing on this as the train rocks from side to side yet moves endlessly forward. What discernible shapes can I make out when looking back on where I've come from?

Yes, there is something visible behind me when I look over my shoulder, certain forms looming out of the fog of memory— the travels, the loves, the marriages. And I'm moving away from all that, I hope, with as much speed as this train putting downstate stations behind it. Onward from now on. And could I invent what I can't remember? And how would this differ from memoir? I would make myself into a character, wouldn't I? In a story about one's life, one would become a kind of fictional character, whether the result was called memoir or a work of the imagination.

And time itself would have a character as well; it would have a flavor and a tang and a shape and a feel. Unlinear, too. Leap-frogging. Arcing over the material of real life like those lucky stones I used to skip along the water. Time: sometimes even turning back on itself as it does in thought.

And history—the world's time—where would personal time and the world's time intersect?

So there's a path of sorts I might take to try this: to re-create the feeling, the emotions of those events, to find the right words. Try it then, at least a sketch. Take a deep breath, and begin.

Glancing now and then out the train window, I see time and memory fusing into something that gives me the illusion of being for a moment at least as solid as the iced-over river road. It's snowing, the wind slanting the thick flakes from west to east directly at the glass that separates me from the rawness of it. I'm going to see my children. I'm bound away, for love of them.

14. MILK BATH

In the center of the room—a high-ceilinged kitchen at the back of the old house—stands a table where the white-haired woman prepares the vegetables for meals, peeling, breaking off stems, slicing. Meat she works on at the large sink, a separate place for meat. Here on this table she set the tin tub that she filled with the warm milk. Calling to the front of the house she waits for her daughter to bring the child.

Her daughter! Nearly a child herself, to give birth at this young age. Dark-haired, big-boned, she had the hips for it. But what did she know about life? She needed her mother on occasions like this. When her daughter came in the woman took the infant from her, holding the child up to her face, cooing at it, making small noises with her lips to match the noises of the babe.

This February child—she needed soothing, she needed protection against the elements outside. The wind howling. The snow falling. The frozen Raritan down the street. The early dark. All these things conspire against a healthy season. Keep the child warm, keep the child in fluids, that's all you can do. Unwrapping her tiny granddaughter the white-haired woman whose wide-cheeked face showed many wrinkles gently lowered the infant into the warm liquid, keeping her broad hand beneath the girl's silky bottom. With the other hand she began to lave the child with milk. Gently, gently she washed each part of her, using her fingers only and a little swipe of a cheesecloth to make clean her ears and the precious parts below.

"Ah-ah, ba-bee," she crooned to the girl as she washed. "Ma-ma is a la-dy . . ."

Fire crackled in the stove. Her daughter watched with the fascination of a novice. Outside the wind howled furiously: times to come, times to come!

ALAN CHEUSE is book commentator for NPR's *All Things Considered*. He is the author of a memoir, *Fall Out of Heaven*; three novels, *The Bohemians*, *The Grandmothers' Club* (reissued by SMU Press in 1994), and *The Light Possessed* (reissued by SMU Press in 1998); and two story collections, *Candace* and *The Tennessee Waltz* (reissued by SMU Press in 1992). His stories and reviews have appeared in the *New Yorker*, *Ploughshares*, the *Chicago Tribune*, and other literary venues. He teaches in the writing program at George Mason University in Fairfax, Virginia, and lives in Washington, D.C.

Neil Adams